Lancaster's Rose

Lancaster's Rose

Karen Hoelscher Johnson

TATE PUBLISHING
AND **ENTERPRISES**, LLC

Lancaster's Rose
Copyright © 2012 by Karen Hoelscher Johnson. All rights reserved.

No part of this publication may be reproduced, stored in a retrieval system or transmitted in any way by any means, electronic, mechanical, photocopy, recording or otherwise without the prior permission of the author except as provided by USA copyright law.

This novel is a work of fiction. Names, descriptions, entities, and incidents included in the story are products of the author's imagination. Any resemblance to actual persons, events, and entities is entirely coincidental.

The opinions expressed by the author are not necessarily those of Tate Publishing, LLC.

Published by Tate Publishing & Enterprises, LLC
127 E. Trade Center Terrace | Mustang, Oklahoma 73064 USA
1.888.361.9473 | www.tatepublishing.com

Tate Publishing is committed to excellence in the publishing industry. The company reflects the philosophy established by the founders, based on Psalm 68:11,
"The Lord gave the word and great was the company of those who published it."

Book design copyright © 2012 by Tate Publishing, LLC. All rights reserved.
Cover design by Allen Jomoc
Interior design by Mary Jean Archival

Published in the United States of America

ISBN: 978-1-62147-460-9
Fiction / Romance / Historical
Fiction / General
12.09.17

Dedication

This book is dedicated to the following persons who encouraged me along the way.

My husband, Charles, whom I woke up in the middle of the night to listen to another chapter I had just completed.

To our daughters—Emily, Erica, Erin, and Elisha—for their support and excitement.

Also, much love and affection to our two beautiful grandchildren—Eden and Isaaq—who are our pride and joy.

Cindy,
As you read this think of the "covered wagon" on your porch.
Karen Hoelscher Johnson

Introduction

The pastels in this book were drawn by my Great-Aunt Carrie Duden. She was my grandfather's favorite sister. Carrie died at the age of eighteen in the year 1909. She was an excellent artist and the book that included these pictures was given to me several years ago. A young woman growing up on the rugged farm scene, she fled to the city of Des Moines where she found a job at a soda fountain. When she died, my grandfather and his father took the buckboard to the capitol city and brought back the body of their loved one. The total distance to Des Moines was sixty-five miles. It was a hot August day. Her body was laid to rest shortly thereafter.

CHAPTER 1

He hadn't been asleep more than a couple of hours when he was awakened by the sound of heavy hoof beats. A familiar voice shook his mind and body awake as he recognized his father's panicky voice. He jumped out of bed and jerked his pants up as his mind began to race frantically. Grabbing his coat as he bolted toward the door, he yanked it open.

"Is Jake with you?"

"No, I sent him home about an hour before sunset!"

"His horse, Lady, came up to the stable almost a half an hour ago."

"What do you supposed happened to him?"

"He probably followed a rabbit or something, and he let his horse get away."

"But he would have walked back to the house or to here depending on which one he was the closest to."

"That's true," offered Jed's father. "But I should have seen him either way because I have covered the entire trail between both places."

"Let me saddle up a horse and take a look."

Ben didn't answer until he was at the door. As he stepped back up on the stoop both men heard the unmistakable sound of a large cat—a cougar.

"Jed, the sound of that cougar may explain why the horse returned home on its own."

"I think we'd better hurry. Bring your horse into the stable so that it can rest after its' run here. You can borrow my other horse."

Jed was now wide-awake.

He tore back into the house and began putting on some warmer clothing, along with two pair of socks and his boots. His father warmed up briefly by the glowing coals of the fire while waiting for his oldest son. A couple of silent minutes passed before they both heard again the big cat's far off scream. Jed hurried even more and grabbed his shotgun and a couple of extra cartridges. Slamming the door behind them they ran to the stable.

"Here, Jed! I can saddle up Sugar while you saddle up your other horse for me."

Ben tethered his horse to a stall and accepted the halter of a fresh horse that his son offered to him. Leaping on their horses, they sped away while watching for tracks of Jake's horse on the snowy trail.

The fresh snow was not deep as of yet, but the wind was beginning to blow lightly. This would be a cause for concern if the horse's hoof prints could not be followed. Unwelcomed thoughts crowded Jed's mind as he desperately watched the trail. *Why had he kept his brother so long? Why hadn't he sent Jake home sooner?* He found no answers as the two men continued to search for more tracks.

The cat that they had heard earlier made no sounds now as they entered the wooded area. Jed and his father knew that not only did they have the cougar to worry about, but the cold and snow as well.

Benjamin interrupted his son's thoughts. "He was dressed warmly. His mother insisted on that before he left the house. I never thought that the horse would leave him, unless something spooked him."

"The horse probably bolted when he sensed that cougar." His body quivered as he thought about the cougar and Jake being out there with it.

They traveled about three-fourths of a mile from Jed's home. They were almost to the wooded area on the neighbor's property.

"Maybe we should wake these neighbors up and they can help us in our search."

Ben mused, "That's a good idea. Do you want me to ride up there and see if I can wake the Wilson boys up?"

Jed returned, "I think that we need some help. We're looking for a needle in a haystack at this point."

Ben reined his horse and pulled on the right tether as he made a motion to head toward the Wilsons' house.

"Whoa! Look there!" Jed pointed to the ground. "I think he went that way."

Following his son's gaze and pointed finger, Ben grunted. "Why would he go through a grove of trees?"

"He must have stopped to chase something and lost track of the time. We better forget about getting the Wilsons and hunt for him ourselves."

"It's a shortcut, but there are some low branches that make traveling through here too dangerous at night. Jake knew that."

"Yes," said Jed. "But Jake is a young kid, and I can see myself doing that when I was his age. I often forgot what I was supposed to be doing when I got distracted."

"I seem to remember you doing this sort of thing when you were a boy, Jed."

For a brief moment Jed glanced at his father and wondered what he was remembering about Jed's childhood antics. If he hadn't been worrying about Jake he might have questioned his father further.

Snow had quit falling as the men and horses picked a path through the darkness. Jed thought they had better find a trail before it started to snow again. He was more disgusted with himself than anything. If something happened to Jake, he would never forgive himself.

"I should have started Jake out long before I did, but I wanted his help to carry in the wood to the lean-to."

Lancaster's Rose

The conversation stopped there as a movement in the tall evergreen caught Jed's eye.

A crack of a branch, with extra weight other than the snow, shook the treetop of the tall pine. The moon came out and plastered the landscape with shadows that laid themselves out on the white ground. An eerie feeling covered the area.

"Jed!"

"I see it."

Slowly Jed dismounted and handed Sugar's reins to Ben. The light from the moon helped Jed to see the cougar as he strained his eyes to see where the cat was positioned.

"About ten feet from the top of the tree, son."

The cat was lying flat in order to be less visible. It was as though he understood that the two men were here to rob him of his prey. He sat watching, and emitted a low rumble from his throat.

"I don't think I have a clear shot. There are a lot of branches in the way."

"Choose it carefully. You may only get one shot. I left my gun back on my horse."

Jed knew that he had to make it a good shot. A wounded cougar could be more dangerous. The men and the animal waited until a couple of minutes had passed before the cat made a move. A nearly transparent cloud covered the moon. It was a waiting game.

The cougar stood about halfway up as though getting ready to jump to the lower branches. At that moment the moon came out from behind the hazy cloud revealing its full light.

"Better take it now, Jed, if you have a clear shot."

There was no response from Jed as he held the gun up toward his face. He felt as though his brow was breaking out into a cold sweat. He wiped it on the sleeve of his coat and drew a bead on the cougar. He thought about what would happen if he missed.

His finger on the trigger, Jed waited only a moment more before saying to Ben, "Hang on to the horses."

Tightening his grip on the halters Ben slowly walked from the tree, speaking gently to Sugar and Prince. "There now, it will soon be over."

At that moment the crack of the rifle told Ben that Jed had taken the shot. The sound of the cat, either jumping or falling from branch to branch could be heard. Jed reloaded his gun.

The cat hit the ground with a thud and attempted to stand on its feet. Jed aimed, prepared to take another shot, but it was soon apparent that the animal's death struggle had begun. He had hit the cougar in the upper chest and saw that already the white snow was turning crimson as the blood seeped from the body and covered the spot where the cat died.

"Good shot, Jed. But we still need to find Jake. He's probably close by. The cat was protecting something."

He's right, thought Jed. *Let's just hope that we can find Jake alive.*

Lancaster's Rose

They were ready to mount up again to pursue their quest to find Jake when Jed noticed several lower broken tree branches off of one of the smaller evergreens.

"It looks as though someone intentionally broke these off as though leaving a trail or something. Do you see that?"

"Yes, I see it, but it appears as if it is only from this tree. Do you see a pile somewhere?"

Both men scanned the area. They had gotten rid of one of the threats but still had the cold to contend with.

"I don't see any tracks but we might have had enough snow to cover up any Jake may have left," Ben offered.

"That's right but we should still see some branches."

"Jed, look over there!"

Jed looked to where his father was pointing and saw a small pile of evergreens. As they got closer to the area, Jed could see a small black boot sticking up out of the snow. There were several drops of blood that led directly to the boot and the branches.

Ben stood slightly back while Jed pulled off the evergreens. There, lying in the snow with his face nearly covered, was Jake. Jed gingerly dusted the light snow off of the boy's face. He touched Jake's face and could feel how cold his brother had already become. He felt under Jake's neck for a pulse and leaned down to put his ear over the boy's mouth. A slight sound was present, but at least he was alive.

"Let's get him to the General Store and get him warmed up."

"Why to the store?"

"That's where your mother is. She felt that she should be doing something and it is halfway between your farm and mine."

Jed easily picked up Jake and walked to where the horses were tied.

Jed handed Jake to his father while he mounted Sugar. He leaned down and took Jake from Ben.

He shifted in the saddle until he felt Jake was in a comfortable position sitting ahead of him on the horse. He opened his coat so Jake could feel Jed's body heat. With his arms around Jake he held the bridle and chirruped for the horse to go.

"Easy, Sugar. We've got to be gentle, but we need to hurry."

Carefully, Jed followed his father out of the wooded area. His horse moved nervously, cautiously skirting the dead cougar.

"I don't blame the horses for being skittish. It must weigh almost one hundred and fifty pounds."

"Yes," Ben replied. "I'd hate to meet up with him without a gun."

Once out in the open, the horses, as though of their own accord, could sense the urgency of getting to Lancaster. The men didn't talk the rest of the way. Jake's safety and well-being was on their minds.

After what seemed like an eternity, the outline of the town's buildings could be seen in the moonlight. The crunching of the horses' feet in the coldness of the night made it seemed

Lancaster's Rose

as if the three of them were the only ones alive. The cold bit Jed's face and the hands that were holding Jake on the horse. The town slept, with the exception of a lone lamp that was shining in the front window of the General Store.

Jed slid off his horse, still holding Jake, as his father tied up the horses at the hitching post. Hardly waiting for Benjamin to open the door Jed nearly fell into the room from the exertion of the activities of the night. A bed had already been placed close to the pot-bellied stove.

"Better get Doc Sherlack. Dr. Mailer is delivering a baby out to the Otterback's," offered Laura, the wife of the store's proprietor.

Without stopping to warm his own hands up, Jed was gone in a flash and easily located the doctor's home. It was one of the four two-story homes in Lancaster. Both doctors had one, as well as the parson. The fourth one had stood vacant for as long as Jed could remember. His feet touched only one of the five front steps and then hammered on the front door. It was only a minute before Doc Sherlack opened the door.

"Doc! We need your help over at the store!"

"What seems to be the problem?" asked the gray-haired man.

"My brother Jake fell off his horse and laid out in the cold for quite awhile before we found him." Why was he explaining this anyway? He needed help for Jake and wanted the old guy to hurry.

No more words were exchanged as Jed hurried the man into a heavy coat. He rushed the doctor back to the store, helping the older man up to the front porch of it. Jed felt like picking up the man whose feet were shuffling.

Goodness, I can see why he isn't helping with the birthing of the Otterback baby, he thought to himself.

Entering the store, Doc Sherlack greeted everyone as he took off his coat and briefly warmed hands.

He sensed the young man's impatience. "You know, if he's cold it won't matter how long it takes for me to check him over. He'll need to get warmed up."

Bending over the youngster, he thumped here and there, took his pulse, and opened and closed the boy's eyelids.

"Well, it is too soon to tell. But someone should stay with him for the rest of the night and keep him warm. I think we'll know more in the morning. Add another quilt to the pile that is there already. I'll stop again first thing tomorrow."

"I think that your father and I will go home," said Jed's mother. "Send for someone if you need help. I'll need to be home in the morning to get the young ones off to school."

Benjamin opened the door for his wife while nodding good night to his son. Laura's husband, Thomas, stoked up the fire and added more wood before leaving the front room with his wife. He, too, nodded at Jed as he shut the door that entered into the family's living space.

Chapter 2

The first couple of hours were spent very restlessly. Jed watched his brother's chest rise slowly but steadily. The color of his face began to change to a rosier hue. He often tossed off the quilts during the night, but whimpered the next moment from the cold.

As Jed sat in the old wooden chair, he continued to berate himself for the events of the evening. Even though the store had a stove, there was a draft that came up from the floorboards and through the poorly sealed windows. He nodded off several times, trying to shift into a comfortable position that might allow him to sleep. The only advantage to that chair was that the arms kept him from sliding to a heap on the floor. More than once his head jerked as his arms slipped off the rests. He wasn't really sure when he got up off of the chair, but as he opened his eyes at first light he noticed that he was on the drafty floor. The sun was persistent as it was beginning to peak through the front doors of the store. Momentarily, he was confused as to where he was. He lay perfectly still as he assessed his situation, realizing that he had a rolled-up blanket that was serving as a pillow. He also felt the comfort of a quilt that he was wrapped up in. Memories of last night snapped his attention back to the present and he cautiously stole a glance next to him where Jake was fast asleep. The color of his face was returning to normal. Jed flexed his arms behind him and cranked his neck both ways in an attempt to work out the stiffness that sleeping on a floor can bring. The fire in the stove had been going all night and he wondered who had been responsible for the comfort of the fire and the quilt. He didn't have too much time to ponder over this as Laura opened the door to his sleeping quarters and greeted him.

"Well, I see that he is looking much better this morning. I think that he was probably more comfortable than you were, although I noticed that at least you had a covering and a pillow of sorts."

"Yes, thank you. I thought that I would be able to stay awake, but I woke up looking at the ceiling and wondering where in the world I was."

"Don't thank me for the bedding. That was of Rose's accord. She'll bring your breakfast in before she heads off to school."

He lay back down on the floor just to rest his eyes when he thought of what Laura had said about Rose. Who was Rose? He had been in this store many times and had never met a Rose or even seen her.

Laura had disappeared into the family's kitchen, and before too long a young girl, about eighteen, entered the room. She looked at Jed, who had gone back to sleep. She stood directly over him with the breakfast tray in her hands. She wondered which was the best way to awaken him was. She thought of tapping his shoulder with her foot but thought better of it as she didn't want to startle him. He might knock the tray out of her hands and that would be a disaster. Instead, she cleared her throat with a soft "*Ahem*." With no response, she repeated this action, a bit louder, and he opened his eyes.

He stared at the full petti-coated skirt and a tray that hid the face of the person carrying it.

He jumped up and as she predicted, nearly knocked the tray from her hands.

"Sorry, I didn't think that I had fallen asleep and you surprised me."

"That's okay. I didn't make much noise as I came into the room. Aunt Laura said that you were awake a few minutes ago."

"I was, but I must have dozed off." When the embarrassment of the situation wore off, Jed was able to look at the pretty young woman. She had beautiful auburn hair that fell in cascades down her back.

She brought out a breakfast that he had not seen the likes of since he had been on the farm with his folks. He tried not to eat like a pig, but suddenly he felt famished and set to filling his stomach, which was feeling quite empty.

She watched him eat with humor in her sweet, brown eyes. He hoped that she would stay a while and keep him company. He ate, gazing at her until he felt her squirming, and he quickly diverted his gaze.

"Laura said that you brought out this quilt for me during the night."

"Yes, I heard the commotion around midnight and peeked into the front room."

"Oh, I hope we didn't disturb you too much."

"No, I had to wait until Aunt Laura came back in the kitchen so I could find out what happened."

"What a night that was! Jake, my brother, didn't come home."

"That's what Laura said. So when I woke up again at two I thought I could go one night without my quilt."

"I hope you didn't give up the warmth of the quilt and go cold yourself."

"No, I just didn't feel right about having a soft comfortable bed while you were sleeping on a cold, drafty floor."

"Actually," Jed said, "I was on the chair for a while, but I must have moved to the floor right after that."

"I saw you on the chair when I came in to stoke up the fire and as I did you roused out of your sleep and shuffled in your chair, trying to get a more comfortable spot. That's when I helped you to the floor and got the quilt off of my bed."

Jed was astonished. "I hope that I wasn't too much for you."

"No." Rose laughed. "You helped too."

Just as he opened his mouth to speak, the store's front door slammed shut as Doc Sherlack clumped noisily through the store.

"Well, I see that he must have made it through the night." He glanced at both of the young people's faces. Feeling that he had just interrupted something, he chuckled to himself and leaned over to check on Jake.

Satisfied that the young lad was going to be all right, he looked at Jed. "I have the buggy out here. Let's take him home and let these people have their store back. Make sure that he is well wrapped. You can have someone return the heavy blankets another time."

Without an opening to ask Rose any more questions, he picked up his brother and carried him toward the door. As Doc held the door open for the young man, Jed turned. "Thanks for the quilt and the breakfast. I'll be seeing you."

Rose smiled and nodded. She turned quickly and headed back to the family's kitchen.

Jed placed his now awakened brother in the buggy and tucked the blankets all around him. He tied his horse to the back of the doctor's hack and squeezed next to the patient and the handles of the buggy. It wasn't too long before Jed realized that the Doc drove his horse the way he did everything else. He drove slowly, but steadily, and definitely in no hurry.

What took a normal person driving a buggy fifteen minutes to the Carlson place took the doctor nearly thirty. Before the horse had even stopped, Jed jumped down and retied his horse to a post near the gate of the house. Jake was comfortably settled in the rocking chair in front of the fire before Doc even made it to the front door.

Doc checked him over again and declared, with rest, that he should be as good as new.

"Mama, are you mad I wasn't here to help with the churning?" asked Jake.

The group laughed. But Jed was not to be turned aside from the fact that Jake had done something that had scared them all.

"Where were you off to last night? You know better than to cut through those trees when there isn't a full light."

Jake hung his head and looked regretful. "I know I did a bad thing and got everyone riled up. I heard a hoot owl in the distance and tried to find out where its tree was."

"Jake, you know cougars come out when the weather is breaking!"

"I know, Jed. I was hoping that when the little ones are born in the spring I could get a baby owl for a pet. But something spooked Lady and I fell off and landed in the snow when she bolted."

"Lady must have sensed the cougar."

"I didn't hear the cat but when I fell off I hurt my ankle and I couldn't get up. So I dragged myself to the trunk of the big tree for shelter. I tried to pull some branches together to light for a fire, but they were too wet to burn."

"It's a good thing you did, Jake. We might not have found you."

"The horse ran away when he heard a cougar. I was so scared that no one would find me before the cougar did."

At this, the doctor pulled up the blankets and examined the ankle. It was an angry purple and hurt to the touch.

"Ouch! That hurts!" Jake grimaced.

"I reckon that this will be sore for a while. It's not broken, but it sure is a good sprain. We'll pack snow around it."

"Will he be able to walk?" Jenny wondered aloud.

"Best that he stay off of it for three or four days. Now, Jenny, if you'll fix me some of that home-cured bacon and some eggs to go with it, we'll consider this bill paid in full."

So, for the first time in several weeks, Jed sat down and had one of his mother's tasty breakfasts. It didn't seem to matter that he had eaten only a short hour ago. Company, even that of an old country doctor's, was welcome when one often sits at a table alone. Listening to the doctor talk about the news of the neighborhood, and of Lancaster, Jed caught up on the news of the town.

"Doc Mailer just delivered Mrs. Otterback's eleventh baby. She's nearly forty and this one was pretty hard on her. He told her husband that the next time she might not fair as well as she did this time. The baby boy was small, but Doc thinks that it will be all right. At least there are a lot of young ones there to help out. They had been hoping for a boy this time so that they would at least have someone to help out on the farm and take it over some day. But I sure wouldn't want to wish ten older sisters on anyone. Anyway, Mr. Otterback said he had his son. He didn't need anymore."

"Goodness!" exclaimed Jed's seventeen year old sister Mary. "I would think that would be enough even if it had been another girl."

Jenny smiled at her daughter and said, "There are some things we can't change. Some men don't feel fulfilled unless they have a boy. Mr. Otterback is one of those men."

"Just the same," Mary returned.

"Did you hear that there's a new blacksmith in town? He's been there for almost a month and is already so busy that he works everyday from dawn to dusk. Even then there are men waiting for him to get there in the mornings to repair some piece of equipment."

"Well, Doc, it's hard to earn a living on these prairies, but it can be done. Most people just have to learn to be patient and work hard because it will take a while to just put food on the table, let alone be successful," offered Ben.

"You know, young man," Doc Sherlack was referring to Jed, "it's about time that you thought about settling down. There's a pack of pretty young girls looking for a good catch."

Jed's ears reddened at the suggestion Doc was making. "I'm taking my time, Doc. There's no hurry."

"You shouldn't wait too long; there won't be many girls to pick from."

"I'll take my chances. I've had plenty of opportunities, but no one interests me."

That was true. Jed had many girls who brought him their fresh breads and baking. He had been tempted, but he didn't feel anything tugging at his heart strings.

"Maybe you're just too particular," Doc added.

Everyone looked at Jed, who said nothing.

"Another thing," added Doc Sherlack, "the family staying at the store with Laura and Thomas are heading out to the Dakotas later in the spring."

"I hadn't heard that," remarked Benjamin.

"Yep, they're looking to start a cattle ranch with another of Thomas's brothers."

"Some settlers are itching to go farther west. Jenny and I are not one of those people. We're settled here, aren't we?"

"Yes, Benjamin, we are." Jenny smiled at her husband.

As the family and the doctor ate and talked, Jed realized that he missed the relaxing conversations that he and his family used to have around the kitchen table. He was thinking of how very pleasant both of the meals he had this morning were. He wondered if, someday, he would have a pretty young wife and children around the table talking and laughing as his family shared their daily meals.

He scanned the homey kitchen with its blue-checked tablecloth and the lace curtains at the window. The care that his mother showed her family each day was evident in her manner and her home. It was more than just four walls, with a group of people living together—it was home. Each meal she prepared was made with love. Jed could not remember when the house was not neat. There was a place for everything and the scene was a pretty picture as the sun peeked its way through the six-paned windows each morning. The sunlight streamed through the glass, leaving patterns on the floor of the cabin.

The fireplace was flickering, and he reminisced back to when he was a boy. He had to turn often to warm his backside, and then his front side in an attempt to keep warm. Very grateful for the home that he had as a young boy, he turned his thoughts back to the present and looked at his parents. He could tell that his parents loved each other a great deal. It was more that just a partnership. It was more than trying to make out a living on a parcel of land. He could see the warmth of his parents' eyes as they spoke to one another. He hoped that someday, with the right spouse, he too, would feel that flame light up his heart and his soul.

Chapter 3

Jed had lingered at the home place longer than he had intended to. The day had dawned bright and beautiful. The sun was still shining with all of its might. Even though it was nearly midday, Jed felt that it certainly must be time to curry the horses, give them their fresh straw for the night, and hurry off to bed. He had experienced a tremendous scare, but his heart was light and his spirit was encouraged as he thought of the events of the previous evening. He tied Prince, the horse that his father had borrowed, to the back of his saddle. He allowed his faithful horse to lead the way home, and as he rode, Jed's thoughts wandered to Rose. Already he was interested in knowing more about her.

He noticed that the stream was beginning to run, tripping over small pieces of ice, not yet melted, that were still an irritation to the smooth flow of the impatient creek. There was crispness within the air that would soon be gone. He couldn't imagine that life could get any better than this. He had a secure home that would support him financially. But, as he was reminded of this morning, he had no one with which to share it.

He wondered when he'd see Rose again. His attention was drawn back to the present when the horse stopped at the barn's small door. He slid off Sugar and led the horses to their stalls.

Jed threw out the old straw and pitched in the new bedding. The aroma from a hot summer day flew across the arc of the path of the pitchfork. It reminded Jed of the months long ago when he labored in the hot sun to gather the wheat. He had placed the straw in the corners of the stable so that they were easily accessible to the horses for their winter food and bedding. Even the horses seemed glad to be back. Jed leaned against the wooden enclosure and reflected over the events of the last twenty-four hours. His attention was pulled back to the present as his horses nickered, wanting to be watered. He grabbed a couple of pails and headed for the creek. He took his time as he lowered the pail into the cold water. Absently, he let the pail slap the side of the creek bank and shower his right leg with nearly frozen water. Again, he lowered the pail, and the second time he was more careful about taking it out of the water. Walking back to the horses, he dumped the water in their trough and gently stroked the horses' manes as they took their fill of the water.

"Sorry, old fellows. I have been sort of lack these days. It seems as if I should be going to bed when I'm really just beginning my work."

Lancaster's Rose

He spent nearly an hour currying the animals, and as he finished he threw a blanket over each one and left the barn, closing the door behind him.

He peered around the homestead and felt a twinge of uncertainty. His eyes scanned the landscape. What was this feeling that he was experiencing anyway? He was so happy when he acquired the land. There had been so much work to do that he hadn't seen anyone, except his father, for months at a time. He didn't mind the work, but at least now he knew what had been missing. The time he had just spent at his folks helped him to realize that.

He thought back to his mother and father as they talked during their meals. Their eyes always looked into one another's as they spoke. They were able to read each other's thoughts without the exchange of words. Their patience and love for one another was apparent as they shared conversations. Even his youngest sister, Sophie, knew that when either parent held her hand at the table it was time for the parent to talk and she had to wait for their attention after they had finished speaking. He wondered if they had always been that way. He thought so, but he probably just began to notice it since he was at the age when it was time to choose a mate.

"Yes," he said aloud. "That is what is missing in my life. I need someone to share it with."

Then, giving his body an awakening shake, he knew he needed to get to work. His day was going to be cut short because of the late start so he decided he would need to pick which chores were most important to complete.

He chose to repair a few of the fence posts that had been snapped off during the January ice storm. He would need to re-dig new holes for them, but he couldn't do that until it thawed. For now, he would just have to be content to wire them up and be ready to replace them when the snow left and the ground thawed. He set about this task, intent on finishing it before dark, but the storm had done more damage than he had originally thought.

He wanted to add some livestock. Two years ago he borrowed the neighbor's oxen so he could work up the prairie sod. The first year's crops on the prairie were always light, but in the second year Jed's crops looked much better. This year would be even more of an improvement. He dug up more trees last fall and would do more early in the spring so that he could raise a bit more corn. Oats would be good as well. If he wanted to add a couple of cows, he would need more straw for bedding and food. Jed had used straw from his father's farm for the first winter. Benjamin was very willing to give it to his son, but Jed felt beholden to his father. He wanted to prove to his family, and mostly to himself, that he could make a living—a good living—off the land on his own.

While there were many things that Jed could do on the farm, there were many things that he preferred not doing. Keeping his small quarters clean seemed to always trouble him. He hated washing his clothes and the dishes. No matter

Lancaster's Rose

how often they were washed, they ended up dirty again. That may have been the big reason for not washing the skillet that he used each morning for his breakfast.

He had no clue on how to do things, such as making soap, although he had often, as a boy, helped his mother with the process. However, he had never done so with the critical eye that was needed for the learning of the task.

Once again, scanning the homestead, he felt satisfied that the place was secured for the night. Extinguishing the lantern, he headed for the shanty.

He fixed himself a supper of salt pork and fried potatoes, and then he dug out the tin washtub and filled it with snow from the side of the house. He hefted it on the hot stove and dug in the clothes box for a clean pair of socks. That was another chore that he had taken for granted. How he hated to wash clothes! He found his other pair. He sure didn't want to put on the same pair he had been wearing for the past few days. Laying them over the back of the chair he had set before the fire, Jed lugged the bathtub to the floor and got in.

Usually, the task of the weekly washing was a quick affair. Tonight, he lay back with his head resting on a somewhat uncomfortable edge. He closed his eyes and thought about the past few days. He couldn't help but think of Rose and how beautiful she was. He was as anxious as a young boy waiting for his father to take him fishing, wondering when he would see her again. *Would she be at church?* As he pondered about what tomorrow might bring, he fell asleep. He woke up and his face felt cold. He realized that he had been asleep for a couple of hours. While the fire was still burning, the water had gotten quite chilly. Thankful that he had laid out a blanket in the warmth of the fire, he wrapped himself in it as he sat by the fire and dried off.

He found his other change of long johns. Usually in the spring, Jed hated to wear them. It was hot with them on, and then the next minute he was glad to have them.

Knowing that he should empty the washtub, he told himself that he would do that first thing in the morning. Happy with that thought, he blew out the lantern and jumped into bed.

He laid his busy brain on his pillow. Facing the fire, he could almost see Rose in the flames. The light that was cast from the fire was just enough for Jed to see the entire room. He would have to be adding onto the shanty if there were to be more than just Jed living here. His parents had a very comfortable home. It was made out of boards, instead of logs, but it also had a parlor and a kitchen with a pantry. Jake and Freddy slept in the room at the top of the stairs. Mary and Sophie slept in the room beyond it. Their room had the stovepipe going through it from the big room below. A circle of light came through the rectangular holes in the metal around the pipe, making interesting pictures on the ceiling. He was going to have to get busy if he were going to have five children fill up the house.

This little card,
I send to you.
To tell you.
I continue true.

Chapter 4

Up slightly before dawn, Jed started the fire in the old cook stove, hoping to warm the shanty up a bit before he came back in from doing chores. At least the chill of the air would be gone. Checking on the horses would be the first order of the day. Methodically, he went through the motions of the routine that he performed each morning and evening. His horses had become his best friends. They had learned to trust him and obey his commands. Jed never lost his patience, nor did he take unforeseeable happenings out on them in any way. They depended on each other. The horses couldn't live without their food and water and Jed needed them to make a living on his farm. Giving them each an affectionate pat, he headed back up to the house.

The fire gave a cheery glow to the room. Even though the cook stove's lids were still on the stove's top, flames snaked out and gave a warm glow to the tiny living area. He pulled a chair up to the stove and warmed his hands, rubbing them together in an effort to bring back the circulation. Still seated, he placed the iron skillet on the top of the stove. He allowed

Lancaster's Rose

it to warm up a bit while he mixed the pancake batter. He was not one to stray from the usual breakfast fare. Soon the cakes were frying. He thought better of the salt pork. Already, he was anticipating his mother's Sunday dinner at the home place. He hoped it would be fried chicken with her mashed potatoes and gravy. No one could beat his mother's cooking.

He had eaten nearly a dozen pancakes before he decided that was enough. No need to bother washing the pan, he'd just use it again for tomorrow's morning meal. That was one of the nicest things about living alone. He could use the same dish for frying the pancakes and for eating them as well. It served as an excellent platter.

Checking his timepiece, he noted that he had nearly two hours to get to the preaching service. That meant he still had plenty of time to get ready. Normally, he was not so careful with getting dressed. But, on this day, Jed wanted to look his best, so he took a little extra care.

It took some time before he could locate his bow tie. The last time he wore it was when Doc Sherlack's wife died. She had developed pneumonia about three years back after she fell outside the house in the winter while drawing water from the well. Her husband was delivering a baby to the Otterback's and she was outside for some time before he found her. Even though she had the best care available, she grew too weak and refused to eat. The doctor didn't blame the Otterback's, but he couldn't bring himself to birth the last two babies that had been born there since the death of his wife.

They buried her in the area on the west side of town. The church was later built next to it. Situated on a small knoll, the tiny cemetery held close to forty graves. This burial place was used for many of the residents of Lancaster that had passed on.

No matter where one looked, the scenery was breathtaking. Glancing in any direction during the springtime, one could witness the hard work of the pioneers and the natural beauty that God had placed there. Tall prairie grasses, along with the wild flowers, stood bending slightly in the gentle spring breezes. Regardless of where one would cast his eyes, the view was a pleasure to behold. If one looked off in the distance toward Jed's, the farmstead was often difficult to spot. It was tucked into the wide valley with three buildings—the house, the horse shed, and the lean-to. One unfamiliar with the area had to know where to find the homestead. But it was there, and Jed was proud of it.

Near the river bottom, a bald eagle could be seen during the late summer and the fall. In the early spring and summer, both of the eagle parents were devoted to raising their young. The parents would push their little eaglets out of the nest in an attempt to teach them to fly. If the little one wasn't ready, one of the parents would swoop down and catch their baby bird on its back. The practice continued until the babies learned to fly.

Jed combed his hair and looked at his reflection in the looking glass. Not bad. He had lost the deep tan that he had acquired in the summer sun. As he studied himself he noticed the keen resemblance to his father. He thought his father a handsome man. Maybe Rose would see that Jed was as handsome as his father.

He pulled out his watch and determined that time had been passing much more quickly than he thought. He finished getting ready, banked the fire, and headed for the door.

Saddling up Prince, Jed threw himself on the big animal's back. He knew that he still had over half an hour to make the three miles to town, so he allowed the horse to set its own pace. It was during times such as these that Jed and his horse seemed to be as one. Prince understood the meaning of each individual nudge of his master. Never had he been hit with a knotted rope or a whip. Jed would lean over the horse's neck and whisper in its ear. That was the only instruction that the horse ever needed.

Traveling on the well-worn path that led to Lancaster, Jed noticed that the stream was running much faster than a few days ago. That was the trouble with spring. One day it could be cold and the next day a warm wind might blow and melt any telltale sign of winter. He was at the end of the two-block main street. Most of the shops were closed for one hour so each storekeeper could attend church. The blacksmith was so busy; he worked all the time. He would only be able to hear the church service on the warm days when the church windows were open.

The storeowners often sold goods when their doors closed for the evenings. In the middle of the night, a knock could be heard at the back door. Men, or young boys, were sent to get doctoring supplies for a sick family member. Pay was not necessary at the time. Families settled up when they could. Storekeepers kept most of the town and the surrounding area on credit. Families paid when the crops came in or when the men were able to work.

Some local residents traded for the things that they needed. Men trapped and sold their furs for the staples that were a must in order to live. Others brought in eggs. Women, who had fewer family members, had a little more time to sew shirts for some of the area bachelors. A few men were carpenters, so when their own work was done they would spend time helping some of the wealthier residents on projects in their homes.

One structure that never seemed to be lacking for customers was Lancaster's single saloon. A cowboy passing through, riders on the stagecoach, or young men with nothing better to do spent their time and their money here. As Jed and his horse walked by that establishment, a young wrangler with too many drinks under his belt flew past the unsuspecting rider and his horse. The bartender, a hefty middle-age man, clapped his hands together and said: "I don't give credit here!"

With a nod to Jed he returned his ample body into the bar and locked the door so he could get to church. As Jed took all of this in, he laughed. It seemed funny that a man who ran a saloon would care about getting to church. He mused that it took all types of people to make up the world.

Lancaster's Rose

At the church, Jed tied his horse to the hitching post and removed his hat. He took up most of the doorway as he entered the sanctuary doors. Sophie, his five-year-old sister, spotted him first.

"Look, Mama, Jed's here!"

Unfortunately for Jed, everyone else looked too. Jed's ears burned as he took a seat behind the already crowded row that was filled with his family. His mother smiled at him and his father gave him a knowing wink. The commotion that Sophie made had distracted Jed, and he forgot to look for Rose as he came in the entryway.

The church was very plain, but it had a dignified and reverent look. A single cross was on the wall in the center of the front near the altar. It was a simple design, but the congregation was very proud of their church. A single bell sounded from the belfry, announcing to the townspeople that it was time to worship. There were no songbooks. There was not enough money left after the church had been built. Perhaps after the social there would be money to purchase them. But for now they had to rely on the women starting them off on the correct note.

As he was pondering these things a female's voice interrupted his thoughts.

"Do you mind if I sit here?" Rose was smiling and looking as if she were a dream.

Not able to answer he scooted over as she sat down next to him. It took a little doing but her full-skirted dress, with petticoats underneath, was finally smoothed down and he looked at her. She was radiant with her hair up and her face a smooth shine. He could not find one fault with her. He hoped that his appearance was pleasing to her as well.

At first when the services started Jed tried to listen to the parson. Parson Jones had no creativity in his dry-as-dust sermon. He often used his boyhood background as examples. Everyone felt sorry for his mother who sat in the front pew with Parson Jones's wife. The mother looked prideful as her son stood in front of the group. She appeared to soak in every word, while the parson's wife seemed a trifle bored with his services.

Most people thought that he must have been a very boring little boy.

Jed had to admit that he didn't enjoy the sermon. He did, however, enjoy the company. From time to time Jed glimpsed out of the corner of his eye to look at the woman seated next to him. She stared straight ahead and didn't look either way.

Finally, services were over and the people stood up and greeted one another. Jed looked at Rose.

"May I walk you home?"

"It is only a short walk, but I would enjoy the company."

Leading his horse by the halter, they walked toward the General Store.

As they leisurely strolled down the dusty street Jed was pondering over a thought that was in his head. "Rose, may I ask you something?"

"Yes."

"When are you leaving for the Dakotas?"

"Not for a while. Mama is going to be having a new baby."

Jed mused, "The rough trail to the west is not place for a baby—a small one at that."

"No, on our way out here last spring, Mama lost a baby."

"Was it sick?"

"No, the roads were so rough that the baby came ahead of time."

"That must have been hard on her."

"It was. Papa promised her that if she had another baby they would stay in one place until it was born."

"Is the baby coming soon?"

"Oh no, she has only carried this one for about a month and a half. It should be born sometime in December."

"So will you leave in the spring?"

"No, we'll be here until the baby is over a year old. Papa will get a job or help in the store."

Jed couldn't hold back the elation that he felt. If he could have jumped over the General Store he would have. He hadn't ever allowed himself to seriously consider that Rose would be here for a while. Now it seemed as if it would turn out all right. What a day this had been!

In only a moment they were at the store. Rose looked at him and said, "Is it okay with you if I stay in town for a while?"

He searched into her brown eyes and wanted to say so much, but the only word he could get out was *yes*.

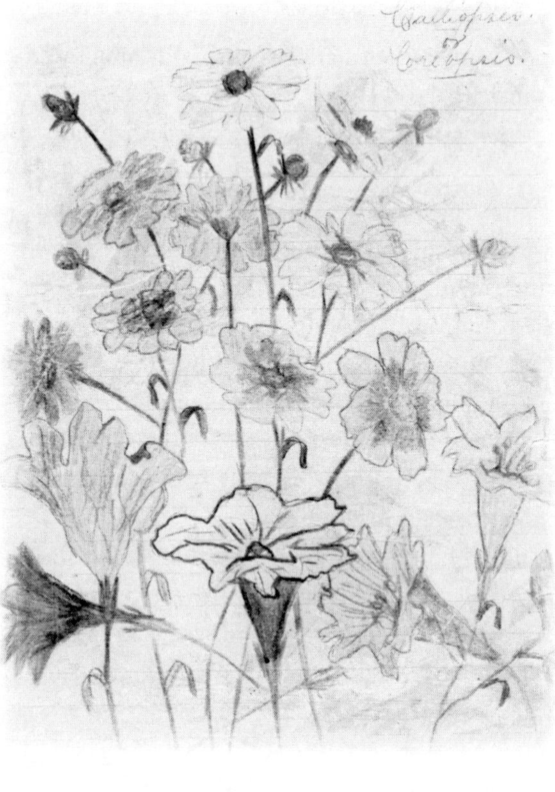
Calliopsis.
or
Coreopsis.

Chapter 5

Now that Jed had actually heard from Rose that she and her family were going to be in Lancaster for another year, each day dawned a little brighter. The setting of the sun seemed to glow rosier, and it appeared as if each sunset was made especially for Jed. The morning sky was bluer than it had ever been. Jed was the happiest that he had ever been in his entire life.

The colors of spring slowly faded into the green of the summer. Jed put in his crops and continued to dream every young man's dream. He became a man with a purpose to every movement he made each day. He and Rose were together whenever there was any type of church or school function. At the lunch box social, Jed made sure he got the lunch Rose fixed. She made Jed's all-time favorite meal of fried chicken and apple pie.

As they sat on a blanket in the shade of the big, oak tree behind the schoolhouse, they looked and acted like a young couple very much in love. A simple touch here and a tender smile there, Jed could feel the same feelings he had seen in his parents' eyes so many times before.

After all the crops were in, there was a singing school for the young adults. Although Jed often sang in the fields or to his horses at night, he didn't sing for anyone else.

Jed rode his horse into town each week for singing school. He tied Prince to the hitching post at the General Store. Then he and Rose would slowly walk to the school where the schoolmaster led them up and down the scales until they were breathless. They learned about the musical scales with the altos chasing the sopranos, the tenors chasing the altos, and the basses running after the tenors. After everyone was exhausted, the evening ended with the young people, in the cool of the night, in breathless laughter.

Afterward, the singers drank apple cider and gathered in small groups to visit.

"I think I will miss singing school," Rose thought out loud.

"I'm not so sure I'll miss the singing, but I will miss our time together."

Jed and Rose were sitting by the stove when Jed's classmate, Henry, invited himself to their twosome. Both Rose and Jed acknowledged him with a nod of their heads.

"Mind if I join you?"

Jed minded. He remembered Henry as an irritation in school. He was not very interesting to listen to and Jed couldn't imagine what he could possibly add to their conversation that he would enjoy. Nevertheless, he nodded for Henry to join them.

"I think that I have never had such good cookies, Rose. Gingersnaps are my very favorite. Come to think of it, Rose, I'll bet you are a pretty good cook. You'll be a great catch some day."

Rose smiled and looked at Jed who had nothing to offer.

"You know, Rose, I don't live far from you. Could I see you home?"

Now Jed thought of something to say. "She came with me and I am walking her home."

"Oh Jed, don't be jealous. Maybe Rose would like to make that choice."

Rose looked at Jed and could see that he wouldn't take much more from Henry.

"No, Henry. Thanks for the offer, but Jed will walk me home."

"How about letting me walk you home next week then?"

Jed spoke up this time and said, "How about never, Henry? Rose isn't interested in the likes of you."

"Jed," whined Henry, "you needn't be so mean. No one likes me."

"Well, Henry, maybe that's because you weren't nice to anyone in the school. You always tattled to the teacher and cried when you didn't get your way."

Henry gave up and slithered away to make a pest of himself to another group.

"That didn't seem very nice, Jed."

"Yes, I know, but Henry is not a nice person. His mother always babied him. He's never done an honest day's work. His father tried to get him to help in the field but Henry's mother always interfered. Besides, I like it with just you and me."

The teacher was blowing out the lamps. Singing school was over with for another week. Jed walked Rose to the store, got on his horse, and headed toward home.

Every Wednesday was not the only time Jed got to spend with Rose. On Sundays there was always church. Somehow they managed to sit together, and often Sophie crawled over the pew's back and plopped herself into Rose's lap. Jed's memories of those days helped him to get through the rest of the week.

As their lives continued to include one another, Jed found invitations for a meal from the General Store came often. In turn, Rose found herself included in the family meal at the homestead of Jed's parents. After a meal, if the weather permitted, the two of them would stroll out of town to the stream where they sat and watched the world go by. Often, they would wade in the cool, clear stream, or throw flat pebbles to see if they would skip through the water. Sometimes they fished and it was more of an annoyance when a fish was caught. They didn't care if they caught anything; they just wanted to be together. It was their favorite spot. It was on these walks and talks each young person shared their thoughts and visions for the future.

Lancaster's Rose

"You know, Jed, I always wanted to be a school teacher."

Jed looked at her in surprise. "Really, I thought you would want to keep house!"

"I always thought I would like that too, but I never found the right man for me."

"That's so hard to imagine that you would have any trouble."

"There was a man once. He was a banker in one of the cities back east."

"That would have been a comfortable life for you, Rose. What happened?"

"That's the trouble. It was too comfortable. I would have had a housekeeper and a maid, but it wasn't for me. Besides I couldn't stand the thought of Mama and Papa going out west. I might not have ever seen them again."

"That would have been hard, but is it possible that you will miss the people of Lancaster?"

Rose smiled. "Yes, that's true—some of them more than others."

With that she held up her face to meet his. He cupped his hand under her chin and kissed her for the first time.

In the warmer days of November, the rustling leaves gently fluttered from the trees and made piles that were heaps of red, orange, and yellow ground cover. Often they could hear a *moo* in the distance from a cow that was searching for the last grass of the fall. They could see how busy the squirrels were as they gathered up the acorns and walnuts in order to prepare for the winter ahead.

Jed's younger siblings begged to be included in these outings. But, even if Jed would have allowed it, Jed's mother, Jenny, would not have. She knew how special this time was for the young people. The golden haze of summer was long gone and more commonly than not, the time that Jed and Rose were together was spent oblivious to the temperature of the day. Time passed quickly for the both of them. When the weather got too cold for a walk, Jed would borrow his father's buggy so that he and Rose could drive as far as twenty miles. They traveled on the well-worn paths that the homesteaders had etched on the ground from the many trips that their horses made going to town or to a neighboring one. The twenty miles back home often took more time, as neither young person was in a hurry to be apart. It was a time that went by so quickly that for two people thoroughly in love, the hours seemed to pass like minutes. Winter was approaching fast, but for now they enjoyed their outings.

"Jed?"

"Yes, Rose?"

"I think that autumn is my favorite time of the year. The outdoors is so beautiful. I love seeing all the animals getting ready for the cold weather ahead."

"It's kind of like people," offered Jed.

"In what way is that?"

"My mother has been busy in the garden storing up the fruits and vegetables, stocking them for the winter. She spends a lot of time preserving enough food to last through the winter and spring."

"That's true," Rose thoughtfully replied. "Mama and Aunt Laura have been busy as well. They keep me busy running errands and watching the pots on the stoves for the preservation process. It is hard work, but I think I could do that on my own."

Each busy with their own thoughts, they lay back down to watch the clouds flit about in the sky. Life was simple at times such as these.

It was one of these occasions that Jed and Rose were sitting on the bank, while the horse grazed, when Jed noticed a horse racing toward them from Lancaster. Jed began to narrow his eyes in an effort to attempt to recognize the rider as the man and horse drew near.

Benjamin pulled his horse to such an abrupt stop that the horse nearly sat down. The older man breathed deeply and spoke to Jed.

"Jed, you had better get Rose back to town."

"What's wrong?"

"Dr. Sherlack and Dr. Mailer are with Rose's mother. The baby is in a hurry to be born. Things are not going well."

Rose gasped and Jed put his arm around her. "It's not time for the baby yet."

"That's so, but Doc Sherlack thinks it will be here by morning. Your father wants you to be there, Rose."

He raced for the buggy and was turning to help Rose in when she passed him in a hurry. She was already settled in before he could offer her his arm.

"Jed, we need to hurry. Papa must be worried if he wants me there before the baby's born."

As much as he dared, he rushed for Lancaster. Although it was only four or five minutes, the trip felt like it took hours.

They pulled up to the store and Rose waited for Jed to help her down. It was as if she were dreading seeing her mother. Looking at Rose, he could tell by her beautiful eyes what torment she was feeling. The hesitation that she felt was partially erased by Jed's gentle squeezing of her arm. She returned the gesture and together they hurried up the steps and entered the store.

Jed's mother was already in the front room. Rose's father, Wilhelm, was pacing back and forth. When he saw Rose, he held out his arms to her. After they embraced she put herself at arms length and, with a questioning gaze, asked, "How's Mama?"

He shook his head and replied, "She's only been in there a couple of hours but she is in so much pain and has lost so much blood already, the doctors are shaking their heads saying that they just don't know."

At that moment the door to the family's quarters opened and Dr. Sherlack came out. Those standing in the room searched his face for any encouragement. There was none.

"Rose, your Mama wants to see you."

Lancaster's Rose

"Oh, Jed! I don't know if I can."

Jed turned her toward him. "Rose, you have got to go in. She needs you."

"Yes, you're right. It's just that it is so hard to see her like this."

"It will be difficult, but you'll be glad that you did. You'll have to be strong for her. You'll be a huge comfort I am sure."

As she hesitated at the doorway she looked at Jed with pleading eyes and said, "You will be here when I come out, won't you?"

At that moment there were a hundred places that Jed would have rather been. However, at that minute, he knew that he would not deny Rose anything. He nodded. Watching Rose close the door behind her, he walked toward the front of the store.

Looking out into the late afternoon, Jed saw that the rest of the town was preparing for the night. Lanterns were being lit in the homes as the arrival of the night began to seep into Lancaster. He stepped out onto the front stoop and noticed how eerie the big, two-story school house was. It was the pillar of the community. Standing in the very center of the town, it loomed over all of the other buildings. He could almost hear the laughter of the children even though there were none present. How long ago those days seemed! He was anxious to get out of school as a young boy. He often thought of excuses to stay home. All he wanted to do was to have his own homestead.

Wilhelm stepped outside to be with Jed.

He broke into Jed's thoughts. "It's a beautiful sight. Back east it was so crowded and the jobs were so scarce that a man felt as if he might suffocate if he stayed there."

"I've never been anywhere but Lancaster, so to me it is home. I can't imagine being anywhere else."

"Your family has been here a while?"

"Yep, father was one of the original settlers of Lancaster. He and his folks got this far west."

"Where is your family from, Jed?"

"Virginia. After the war was over my father said the beauty of the south was gone. He worked in Richmond. He came here with his folks and shortly after that intended on going as far as Oregon to find land through the Homestead Act."

"What made him settle here?"

"His mother became ill and died very suddenly. Grandfather didn't have the heart to go on, so he and my father stopped here and became one of the first settlers in the area. The town wasn't even platted yet."

"Is the land where your father homesteaded the farm he is on now?"

"That's right. He married my mother about a year later. I really don't know about her family. They were from out east somewhere, but her parents were never here."

The conversation stopped at this point as both men turned toward the front door. Rose was stepping out of the porch.

"Rose, how is she?"

Lancaster's Rose

"Very tired. She asked for you, Papa."

At this Wilhelm left the young people and went to see his wife.

Rose and Jed sat on the front step and threw a blanket, which Rose had carried with her, over their shoulders. She looked at the stillness of the night before she began to speak to Jed.

"When I went into the room, Mama looked so tired and weak. I waited a moment until she opened her eyes. She wanted time alone with me."

"Can you tell me what she said?"

"Yes. I don't think she'll mind sharing it with you."

"Was she worried about something?"

Rose's eyes filled with tears as she nodded. She waited a moment or two until she composed herself. "Mama took my hand and squeezed it and told me how much she loved me."

"Rose, I'm glad you went in to see her."

"I am too, Jed. She asked me to do something for her." She paused.

"What did she want?"

"She asked me to raise this baby as if it were my own if something happened to her."

"What about your father?"

"Oh, he would help too, but she said that men don't have the mothering instinct that a woman does."

"What did you tell her?"

57

"What else could I tell her? I would love this baby no matter what. I always thought I would help Mama with it, but I want her to be there too."

Jed pondered what Rose had told him and wondered how he would fit into this plan. He had decided in his heart that he and Rose would be married. This would complicate things but he was willing to do anything to be with Rose.

Rose put her head on Jed's shoulders and cried. He didn't know what to say so he said nothing. For the next hour as the moon was easing itself into the night sky, Rose slept, leaning against Jed's shoulder. As he sat there, he noticed Sugar was at the hitching post and the buggy was gone. His father has taken the buggy home and had gotten Jed's horse for him. He hadn't noticed the exchange.

His shoulder began to ache from being in one position for that much time. When he thought he would have to shift and moved into a more comfortable position, Rose woke up.

"Do you feel better?"

"Yes, I should go check on Mama."

As Laura came through the front door to offer Rose and Jed a bite to eat, sounds from Rose's mother crying out could be heard the back room.

"No, thank you, Mrs. Fallman, but I must be going. My animals on the farm will think that I have neglected them. I've been away for quite a while. Rose, I've got to go."

"Thank you, Jed, for being here. I don't think that I could have made it without you."

Lancaster's Rose

He answered with a smile, kissed her on the forehead, and strode toward his horse.

"I'll be back first thing in the morning. Your Mama will be all right. I can feel it."

Rose waved as he left and she and Laura walked back into the store together. Jed could hear the cries from Rose's mother as he tugged on the reins of Sugar.

"Let's go, girl."

The moon offered a light for Jed as he headed toward home. He could see the serenity of the night. All lights in Lancaster had been blown out for the night. The tall trees appeared as if they were listening to the coolness of the evening. A lone call of a cow in the distance mooed out in a barnyard. He noticed the cold setting in and pulled up the collar of his jacket. Yes, winter was coming. It had been so pleasant sitting by the stream earlier in the day and now the winter was beginning to make its' presence known.

Jed turned up the lane to the stable and readied things for the night. Prince whooshed a greeting to the Jed and Sugar. Lighting a lantern, Jed cleaned out the stalls and threw in some new straw as bedding. Going to the granary he scooped up a bucket of oats and gave each animal its share. Fresh water had to come from the creek and as each horse required two buckets, it took a couple of trips.

Satisfied that his animals were cared for, he fastened the stable door and strolled toward the shanty. The stove was cold as he had been away since late this morning. He thought he would just crawl into bed when he decided that a fire would take the chill off of the evening. He chose to forego his meal and hit the sack. As he lay there watching the little flames escape the small slots in the bottom of the stove, Jed thought about the events of the day. What if something happened to Rose's mother? Would they still go out west or stay here? He wondered if Rose would feel obligated to stay with her father and help with the baby. She did promise her mother that she would. Finally, sleep overcame him and his busy brain shut down for the night.

The next morning Jed woke up at the crack of dawn. He quickly dressed without bothering to stir up the fire. There would be no breakfast today as he was in a hurry to get back to town.

Entering the stables Prince greeted him with a snort. He was anxious to get his morning oats while Sugar slept on. Poor thing, thought Jed. She's tired from last night's late ride. Again watering the horses and pitching them new straw, he turned to get the saddle for his horse then thought better of it. He would take Prince. He would enjoy the exercise and Sugar would enjoy the rest.

Picking up Prince's saddle he noticed that the under belly strap was broken. Irritated, Jed wondered when that happened. He thought back to the night he and his father rode through heavy brush looking for Jake. It must have caught on some branches and broke. Now he would have to take the time and repair it.

Going back to the house he found another buckle that he could use to repair the strap. Once back in the stable he found the tool that he needed in order to fix it. The longer it took him the more irritated he got. He tried to hurry too much. He made mistakes in his effort to rush the process of repairing the saddle strap. It took nearly an hour. By the time he got along the trail the sun was halfway up in the sky indicating that it was mid-morning. Rose must have been wondering what was taking him so long.

Jed urged Prince to a quick gallop. He normally would have noticed the scenery around him but today he had one thing on his mind. As he arrived in Lancaster, the shops were already opened and waiting for business. The blacksmith waved an arm in greeting without looking up from his work. The saloon was already sporting a good trade that early in the morning. He saw the parson who reminded Jed about services on next Sunday.

At the General Store, he tied Prince to the hitching post and hesitated, wondering what he would find inside.

The front door opened and Wilhelm stepped out.

Rose's father came out to greet him and said, "The baby is here. She is small, but not too small. The doctors said it will live. But"—his voice cracked—"Susan is very weak. The doctors will take turns staying with her and the baby for the first few hours. Your mother has offered to stay and for that I am grateful. Dr. Mailer told her to go home though and to come back to help Susan later. It's too early to tell. At least they both survived the birth."

"Where's Rose?"

"She's waiting to go see her mother. The doctors needed a few minutes with her."

"When was the baby born?"

"About forty minutes ago. It was a very difficult night. Rose slept off and on. Susan wants Rose to name the baby. She always felt badly that she had no brothers or sisters to play with during her childhood to keep her company."

After only a few minutes Laura stepped out on the stoop. "Jed, I'm glad you're here. Rose wants the both of you to come inside."

At this both men entered the building and waited for Rose to come out of the living quarters. It wasn't long before she came into the front room.

"I want you all to meet my little sister, Hope Elizabeth Fallman."

She held the baby out for Jed to see and he could spot the resemblance, as little as she was, to her big sister. The infant was red and wrinkled. He smiled at Rose's evident love for her baby sister.

"Jed, would you like to hold her?"

Jed declined Rose's offer to hold Hope, fearful she might break. How does Rose manage to hold the little baby and look as if she enjoys it? She cradled the baby next to herself.

"Jed, have you ever seen anything more precious than this baby?"

Lancaster's Rose

He didn't know how to respond. It was awfully small and just a twist of auburn hair. He didn't think that she was particularly pretty, but he sensed that this was not the time to say what he thought. He simply nodded at Rose's words.

Still cradling the baby, Rose returned her to their mother in the small bedroom. Laying Hope in the crook of her mother's arm, she kissed her on the forehead. The weary mother fluttered her eyes open acknowledging that the bundle had been placed beside her and drifted back to sleep.

Rose continued to sit with the pair and, finally lying beside her mother, she dropped off to sleep. She didn't hear the bedroom door open as Wilhelm peeked in to look at his family. Not wishing to disturb them he quietly closed the door and returned to Jed.

"You might as well go home, Jed. They all need to rest and Rose will sleep better if you're not here. She's behind a night's sleep."

Jed knew that Rose's father was right, and he had chores to tend to. As he was getting ready to leave, Laura came out of the kitchen.

"Jed, we're just going to sit down to some breakfast. Would you care to join us?"

As he was about to turn down the offer he thought better of it. He was hungry and he wouldn't mind the company.

"You know, I think that I'd like that, Mrs. Fallman."

So heading into the living quarters, Jed sat down at the family's table to enjoy a breakfast that tasted like his mother's home cooking. He had never thought about what the living quarters looked like. He came in the store to purchase what he needed. Now, he glanced around at the coziness of the kitchen. It had one window on the east wall and one on the west. The stove sat nearly in the center of the room, and one had to go behind it in order to reach the back cupboard. The wash stand was under the east window and the rest of the room was very basic. A table and two benches were toward the west wall with a chair at the end for Thomas, Laura's husband.

As they ate the conversation turned toward the topic of Lancaster.

"Jed, what do you know about this town? What made the settlers plat this area?" Rose's father asked.

"Well, the railroad was supposed to come through here, but it ended up farther to the south. Spectators bought a bunch of the land, in fact, they bought the whole area that would become Lancaster and made profit on the lots they sold. They knew what they were doing because the area around Lancaster hadn't been homesteaded except by a few people."

"I noticed that the businesses seem to be doing a pretty fair trade."

"Yes, we have had a few of them pick up and leave, but for the most part people have been staying. Because of the large amount of businesses a new schoolhouse was needed. They built the two story one about two years ago. There's another one just like it about few miles to the west."

"It seems to be the hub of the town."

Lancaster's Rose

"Yep, pretty much everybody comes to Lancaster when there is a social doing here."

"Rose is finished with her schooling. Her mother is going to need her help with the new baby and such. I'm looking to move in Doc Sherlack's mother-in-law's cottage. Thomas said she died about ten years ago and he wants to sell the place. He wanted to sell it when the wife was still alive but she couldn't bear to part with her mother's memories. It sat for seven years and when Doc. Sherlack's wife died he had trouble parting with it because of his wife."

"I'm not sure I know where that is."

"Why, it's just on the edge of town. You can see it from the church."

"I hadn't noticed it, I guess. I had better get moving. Thanks for the breakfast, Mrs. Fallman. Please tell Rose I said goodbye."

"I will. See you soon, Jed."

With that he entered into the front room and was out the door and on his horse heading toward home. As he rode in the brisk morning Jed saw the things that he had missed on his journey into town. The trees were all bare and it seemed as though they were undressed for the coming of the cold weather. The ground was all brown and the leaves blew across the well worn path. The sun was trying to peak out from behind the clouds. He was thinking about the jobs that he needed to get done for the winter. He had better be repairing the leak in the horse stable. It would probably be all right for the winter, but by spring it would need some new tar paper so the rain wouldn't get in.

Back at the farm, Jed cared for his animals. He then prepared to fix the roof of the stable. Finding the tar paper and the necessary tools that he needed for the job, Jed set to work with a happy heart. The hole was larger than he had anticipated so he was on the roof for nearly half a day. Once he was finished, he fed and watered the horses and curried them in the growing darkness of the day. As he closed the stable door for the night, he noticed that the hinges were loose. Thinking about the wolf he had heard two or three nights ago he concluded that he had better fix them. Usually, wolves didn't bother coming up so close to where the people lived. But, the buffalo were gone from the prairie and the wolves became bolder because of their hunger and would creep up to the buildings at night.

Satisfied that the horses were safe within their walls, he headed toward the house. A fast movement caught his eye. He peered into the twilight of the night and thought he saw a shadow. Staring into the darkness he dismissed his thoughts and locked the door to the house for the night.

Once inside he threw off his jacket and prepared to get his supper. It was then he noticed that he was out of wood for the stove. This was the time in his life when he was not glad to be on his own. His mother would have had supper ready and now he needed to choose whether to get wood or go without

Lancaster's Rose

his evening meal. Being independent had its advantages, but making meals was not one of them.

Heading out to the woodpile he heard the nervous whinny of one of the horses. He'd check on them in a minute, but first the wood.

Reaching down he picked up an armload and felt a pair of eyes looking at his back. Slowly turning around, he didn't see anything. He shrugged the feeling off, but he remembered the sound of the horses just a moment ago. Moving toward the house he sensed more movement behind him and turned to face a buffalo wolf. It was an old one obviously not well enough to make the annual pilgrimage to the pack's winter hunting grounds.

Without his gun Jed knew that he was in trouble. He was still twenty or so yards from the house and the old hungry wolf showed his teeth to Jed.

"This is not a good time to panic," Jed said aloud.

He dropped a piece of wood as he sidestepped toward the house. The movement temporarily distracted the wolf. It drew back slightly.

Jed flung another piece of wood at the wolf, who was taken aback by the strange weapon. *At least it frightened him. Now we're both scared,* thought Jed.

Still ten yards or so from his front door, Jed wondered if he had enough of the strange weapon to make it to the house. Clearly irritated, the wolf tried to position itself between Jed and the door. Another hunk of wood slammed into its nose, dazing it just long enough for Jed to dash for the house. Slamming the door shut behind him, he leaned against it and took several deep breaths before he heard the wolf sniffing at the base of the door.

Hearing the horses again Jed knew that the wolf had to be shot before he got a trap set. He looked out the window toward the stable and saw that there was a full moon. He could also see the wolf trying to bite through the stable walls. It found where one of the boards was rotting at its barn's base.

"For an old wolf he's got a lot of ambition." Jed mused aloud. Loading up the shotgun he thought better of it and took his rifle instead, thinking that he would get a better shot if the wolf got too close to the horses.

He donned his jacket while still looking out the window at the wolf. Thinking that he had better sneak up as close to the wolf as possible, he quietly eased the door shut and a slight click could be heard as it latched.

Hoping to get close enough to the wolf before he was spotted, Jed hid behind trees as he traveled toward the stable. As he dodged behind the last tree, the wolf looked warily toward the house. Satisfied that he was alone, he pursued his quest.

Jed raised his rifle and took aim at the unsuspecting animal. Ready to pull back on the trigger Jed stepped on a twig that snapped under his weight.

Alerted, the wolf eyed the tree where Jed stood and sensed the danger. It took a step back and fled as Jed took a shot.

"Did I miss him?" he thought out loud. Reloading as he took careful strides, he crept toward the stable. The sound of the gun must have frightened the horses as Jed could hear the sounds of their hooves pounding on the hard ground in their shed. Once he reached the shed he peeked around its far side to see if he had shot the wolf. Seeing nothing, he began to doubt whether he had hit his target at all. The sound of a quiet snap caused Jed to whirl around just in time to see the wolf ready to spring. Raising the gun to his waist Jed didn't have time to aim. He shot as the wolf leapt toward him. The wolf landed on Jed, who under the weight of the animal was knocked down and temporarily pinned beneath it. Jed rolled the wolf off of him and sprang up, still holding his gun.

The ground was already showing the blood seeping out from the wolf's body. Jed shook visibly for several moments before collecting himself and poking his gun into the wolf's side.

"Well, that was close enough," he spoke to the wolf.

Leaning the rifle up against the stable he dragged the wolf by its tail to the back of the shed. He checked on his horses, speaking to them to calmly, and refastened the stable door. Grabbing his gun he headed toward the house and picked up pieces of wood as he walked.

Back in the house he made a quick supper and went to bed, exhausted by the exertions of the day. Jed closed his eyes and fell into a deep sleep.

"Cherries"

CHAPTER 6

Jed and Rose's courtship could be compared to no other. Rose often rode out to the farm to offer an opinion about a project that Jed was working on. She was especially interested in the changes that were being made to the house. Not that they were extensive or expensive ones. That would not have been a necessity. They were simple ones that Jed valued Rose's thoughts on. Even adding a tree or two in the yard was well thought out. It was difficult for him to plant trees. He had spent so much time clearing his land of all the trees, brush, and brambles that he was hesitant to add anymore. But Jed was finding out that Rose loved nature and making things beautiful, and he loved Rose. Already in the middle stages of their courtship, Jed knew that there was nothing that he could ever deny Rose.

Life had developed into a pattern. Each Sunday they met at the church, saved a seat for the other person, sat together, and then went to Rose's home or Jed's parents' home to have dinner.

One Sunday afternoon, when summer was well on its way, Jed and Rose took Benjamin's buggy out to Jed's homestead. He wanted her to see how the trees they had planted were growing. He knew that she loved baby animals and he wanted her to see the chicken coop that he had made. He also wanted to show her the mother hen and her twenty baby chicks.

At first she didn't see the little house and her surprise was even better than Jed had expected.

"Oh, Jed! Look at them! They are so cute!"

"I never really thought of baby chicks as cute—just good eating when they grew up."

"Eating? You can't possibly eat them! You can use them for eggs."

Jed thought of all the grain it would take to keep these just for the purpose of having eggs. "Rose, the hens are always eaten when they get old."

"That seems so cruel, Jed."

"Perhaps so, but that is the cycle of life here on the farm."

"I'd rather not think of that right now."

"Rose, come here and sit on the stoop with me. I want to show you something."

"What is it?"

"When your mother had Hope, I was talking to your dad about my grandparents coming out west."

"I didn't know you and Papa talked."

"Yes, it was the day that Hope was born."

"He never said anything about it."

Lancaster's Rose

"Yes, I told him my grandma died here so that's why my father and grandfather settled here in Lancaster. She and grandpa were raised in Richmond and Grandpa had a good job, so they were rather wealthy before the war started. After the war they had to sell most of their belongings in order to buy what they needed to start a new life out west."

"I never heard your father speak of his parents."

"That's right, the memories of his mother made it hard for him to speak of her," said Jed. "My father said Grandpa was heartbroken when she died and gave up his will to live."

"That must have been so sad for him."

"I think that it was, but he got a claim and homesteaded 160 acres."

"What did you want to show me, Jed?"

"Right before she died she took her wedding band off of her finger and clasped it momentarily before she handed it to my father."

"That had to be difficult to take it from her."

"He said he would never forget how her tiny hands clutched that ring. She gave it to him and told him to save it."

"That seems to be a strange request!"

"Not really," Jed chuckled softly, "because here's the rest of it."

"What did he do with it?"

"Grandma had requested to her son that he give it to her oldest grandchild—his oldest child."

"Father gave this to me a couple of months ago along with her request."

"I see, Jed."

"Do you, Rose?"

She looked at him with her brown eyes and auburn hair that was blowing in the summer breeze. "I think so. But tell me so I know for sure."

Jed stepped off the stoop and bent down on his right knee. "Rose, I want you to be my wife. I can't think of anyone that I would rather spend my life with. I want you to be my helpmate and the mother of my children and to grow old with me."

Rose couldn't speak as tears glistened in her eyes.

"Say that you'll marry me, Rose."

"Yes, Jed. I'll marry you."

He placed it on her third finger then pulled her close and they kissed, confirming their love and their promise to one another.

"Jed, it is beautiful! I can't wait to show my mother."

"Are you happy, Rose?"

"I couldn't be more so, Jed."

"Then leave it in and in a couple of months we'll be married."

The rest of that afternoon they began to make more plans for their life together. From that moment on, Jed conferred with Rose regarding improvements he wanted to make on their farm. She wanted a clothesline on the side of the house.

He thought it would look better if it were in back of it. Before long, Jed was digging holes for where Rose wanted it.

She wanted to have a little porch on the front of the house so that they could watch the sunset in the west. Jed and Benjamin built one and placed a railing around it and made three broad steps leading up into the house. Wilhelm and Thomas came out one Sunday and built a swing for Rose. She planted flowers of all sorts. She especially loves the daisies. Each day was a joy for them as they prepared for their new life together.

A small bedroom was added to the back of the house. Rose wanted a window on the east and on the west sides. She wanted to see the sun rise and set on their little home. It was a perfect house for two young people to call home.

Things couldn't have looked better. There were planning on being married at the parsonage.

"Jed, I saw Mrs. Wenter the other day. She said back in the east, fashionable couples get married in the church."

"I thought we were happy about being married at the Parson's home."

"Yes, we were. But she said that the west is so rough and such a God-forsaken country."

Oh brother, thought Jed, *Mrs. Wenter sure has strange ideas.*

Rose continued, "She told me in the east people would look down their noses at you if you weren't married in a church."

"Did you tell her we were happy with our plans?"

"Yes, but you know how persuasive she can be. She said that I simply have to think about how it would look. It would appear as if we were ashamed to marry each other by sneaking into the parson's home."

"And what did you tell her?"

"I told her that I don't think that at all."

Jed was getting mad at Mrs. Wenter just listening to the conversation.

"And she said?"

"And that is just it, child, you aren't thinking. Imagine how pretty it would be to have flowers all over the church. The ladies are anxious to share their flowers."

He looked at Rose. "I just want something simple. The main idea is for us to be married. We can do that without a big fuss."

"Yes," Rose returned, "but don't you think that it would be nice to have our families there watching? The parson's home is much too small for our families."

Jed could tell by looking at Rose that she wanted to be married in the church. He bowed his head and nodded his approval.

"She is planning on the first of next month." Rose smiled her beautiful smile and they continued with their plans of the homestead.

It was the very next Sunday that Jed rode up to the church. He hopped off Prince and tied him in the shade. Everything

Lancaster's Rose

was right about this day! After church they were going out to Jed's parents to make plans for the dinner after the wedding.

Jed dashed inside and looked for Rose and her family. He was so late that he couldn't imagine why she wasn't there yet. Then as he scanned the rest of the benches, he noticed that his family was strangely absent. As his eyes continued the search he noticed that there were several people watching him. Why were they looking so seriously at him? Where was Rose?

Stepping back outside the church, he scanned the town for an answer. Dr. Mailer's buggy was out in front of the little cottage that Rose and her family had moved into when they had decided to stay in Lancaster.

Long strides quickly brought Jed to the front door. Without thinking, he grabbed the handle of the door with such earnest that he nearly jerked the door off the hinges.

"Rose!"

Jenny and Benjamin were sitting by Rose, holding her hands. All three looked up as Jed knelt next to the small circle. He could tell she had been crying.

"What's wrong?"

"It's my father. You know he had been feeling poorly for the last few weeks. Last night, around midnight, he got worse so I went to get Doc Mailer. He doesn't know what is wrong with him. We're not even sure he will live."

Benjamin got up and gave his chair to his son. Jed quickly put his arm around Rose's shoulder, and she placed her head on his chest and sobbed. He didn't know what to say so he held her and said nothing.

Jed stayed with Rose for the rest of the day. He would have sat up with her all night just to be with her, but her mother sent him home so Rose could get some rest as well. She was right. He needed to get home and tend to his animals. He didn't want to leave her. With a promise that he would return first thing in the morning, he said good-bye and left. The ride back to the homestead was long and Rose's worry continued to plague his thoughts. He could take any kind of pain and worry as long as it concerned him but he hated it when Rose had to bear the brunt of it. It was a good thing that his horse knew the way home because Jed's preoccupied mind gave no signals to the animal.

It was well after midnight when Jed finished his chores. He felt no hunger as he prepared to turn in for the night. As the weather had turned warm, he left the door open with the mosquito netting covering the doorway.

He could hear the sounds of different animals in the distance. It had been a fruitful spring. Rain had been plentiful and the wheat had made a good stand. Off in the far away trees he heard the hoot of an owl. Closer to home he listened to another owl answering it. In his own home he listened to the horses whinnying good night to each other in the stable.

Before long he would be sharing these sounds with Rose. Happy in that thought, he rolled over on his back and promised himself that whatever Rose was facing with her

Lancaster's Rose

father he would be there to help. Shutting his eyes, he fell asleep and drifted off into dreamland.

In the morning Jed hurried through his chores and headed into town. There was no change in Wilhelm. After he had checked on Rose and helped her in any way possible, he returned to his farm and mindlessly performed the tasks that he had set for himself to get done that day.

His pattern of each day had been set and although the dawn broke daily with a beautiful promise of good things to come, Rose's father was failing. On one bright and clear morning Jed rode into town to see Rose. He noticed a wagon outside of the Fallman's home. He couldn't imagine what might have happened. He feared that Wilhelm might have died during the night.

"Rose, what is happening here?"

"Oh, Jed! They're taking father to go back east."

"Why out east?"

"They think the doctors there can help him. Mother's got a man hired to take them back in the wagon."

"Rose, this doesn't make any sense. It's so sudden!"

"I have to go with them. It just wouldn't be proper for them to go alone."

"No, Rose, stay here. We're to be married this week and we'll have Hope with us. Your parents can come back when your father gets well."

"No, Jed, I need to go with mother."

"But, Rose." He stopped. He knew that she was right. "How long will you be gone?"

"Until he gets well and his strength returns."

"Let me go with you."

"No, Jed. You are a dear for wanting to, but you need to take care of the homestead so that when I come back there will be a place for us to begin our life together."

"When are you leaving?"

"As soon as possible. They're afraid that if we wait any longer it will be too late."

Jed glanced at the wagon. A few of the family's essentials had already been placed in there. A space just large enough for a man to rest had been left toward the front of it. The old wagon would not be comfortable to ride in, but it would be better than by horseback.

After a few more personal items had been added and enough food to last a week or two had been included, they would leave.

"Jed, do you have time to take me out to our stream just for a few moments?"

Without answering her, he brought up his horse, helped her on, and mounted up behind her. The ride to the water's edge went much too quickly. Few words were exchanged. The chance to be together was enough. As they sat next to one another, he put his arm around her and she leaned her head on his shoulder.

"Jed, I want to thank you for all that you have done for me."

Lancaster's Rose

"What do you mean, Rose?"

"Whenever I had a problem you have always been there for me. I could have never made it through Hope's birth without you."

"You've made my life more than a dream. I have hope for a life with a person that I love more than anything on the earth."

"Jed, I have a confession to make. Do you remember when I asked you for the clothes line?"

"Yes.

"Well, you wanted to put it behind the house and I wanted on the side."

"I remember. What about it?"

"I really wanted it in the back too."

"You did? Why did you want me to put it where I did?"

Rose giggled before she went on. "I just wanted to see if you would let me have my way."

Jed laughed. "You know I wondered about that but I love you so much that I would have put it on top on the stable if that's what you wanted."

"We've made some wonderful plans haven't we, Jed?"

"Yes, and when you come back we'll finish those plans after we are married."

They sat for a few minutes more holding each other forgetting only briefly of what was going to happen in the next few minutes.

She leaned forward, kissing him, and he returned it with great passion.

"We had better get going. We're leaving as soon as we get back."

"Don't forget me, Rose."

She smiled at him and let him help her back on the horse. The ride back went by swiftly. They savored their last moments together. Lancaster quickly came into their sight. Rose's mother was stepping into the wagon. Jenny handed Hope up to her. They saw Rose and Jed close by.

Helping her off the horse, he held her for a long moment. As he looked into Rose's eyes he felt his heart beat faster. It felt broken as he thought of her leaving for any amount of time. He held her and then helped her into the wagon. She tried to smile through her tears.

"I'll write when I am able to." Bravely, she looked back once.

He turned from the direction that the wagon was moving and numbly aimed his horse toward home. How would he ever keep going? What was he going to do without the hope of going through the day and seeing Rose?

CHAPTER 7

If anyone had gone out to Jed's place in the months to come, they would have been sure that he had lost his mind. The work that he had done before was nothing compared to the way he worked now.

Obviously, the thing for him to do would be to work as if Rose were still there. Together they had talked about some of the changes they made to the house. He had built on an extra room to the east, which was to be their bedroom after they were married. She had offered suggestions regarding the new addition that Jed had never even thought of. It seemed unnecessary for some of these changes, but he wanted her to be happy.

Obsessed with the thought of Rose, he continued to work himself nearly to death. Laboring for eighteen hours and then sleeping for the other six became Jed's pattern. In all fairness one couldn't say that he slept all of those six hours. He would lie awake trying to make his mind rest. When he couldn't sleep, he got up early. He sat on the porch swing in the moonlight. Rose loved to sit out on the small porch and watch the sun begin to set.

Lancaster's Rose

Over four months had passed since the Fallman family had left for the east. One sunny afternoon Jake rode up to Jed's farm. He carried with him a message from their mother.

"I got sent here to tell you that the mail will be coming to Lancaster sometime around mid-afternoon. Ma thought you might want to come here to town to see if there is a letter from Rose. When is she coming back, Jed?"

"Soon, I hope. Soon."

Jake didn't even dismount his horse. Jed was on his way to the barn to saddle up Prince. With a quick, easy motion, Jed was on the animal's back and heading for the road. Chirping to the horses, the two brothers were headed back to town.

Although the day was beautiful, Jed couldn't take the time to enjoy it. He was perturbed for allowing himself to hope for a letter. He needed to know how Rose was.

As they pulled into Lancaster, a small crowd was waiting at the General Store. By observing the others, Jed knew that the mail was in. Each man had to wait his turn.

Finally a letter from Rose was in Jed's hand. Mounting his horse, he flew down the road clutching her letter in his hands. He stopped near the creek, at their favorite place, tied Prince to a willow branch and sat under a willow tree to read her letter. Anxious to read it, he nearly tore the letter in half. Even as he opened it, he hesitated briefly. Somehow he knew that this letter would very closely affect his future with Rose. He had felt such love and longing for her that he took a quick breath before he could even read her words. Though he felt uneasy, he began to read the letter in earnest.

Dearest Jed,

It seems as if so much time has passed since we have been together. I miss the people of Lancaster, but I especially miss you. I need to tell you that Father died about a month ago. Mother is inconsolable and is having health problems of her own. She suffered a stroke about a week after Father died. Her left side is totally paralyzed and she remains bedridden. The doctors don't expect her to get well, but she could be like this for years, and I have Hope to think of. In short, my dearest Jed, I will not be coming back to Lancaster. My mother cannot be moved and I cannot leave her. My heart remains with you, and I will get through all of this with my memories. I'll remember the home we would have shared, our plans for the future, but most of all I shall never forget your love. The time we spent together and our little special place by the stream shall help me face the rest of my life without you. Although I truly believe we were meant to be husband and wife, it will have to be in spirit only. Remember that I love you and will carry my love for you in my heart forever.

Yours,
Rose

Sometimes dreams aren't meant to be lived. Perhaps they are meant to be exactly what they are called—dreams. In one letter, Jed's hopes, expectations, and plans for the future had

Lancaster's Rose

gone up in a cloud of smoke. A piece of Jed's heart went up with it—a piece that would never return.

He folded up the letter, shoved it into his coat pocket, got on his horse, and headed home. As Jed headed up the path to his farm, everything looked different—empty, deserted. The dreams and the hopes that he had in his heart, the ones that had kept him going for over a year, were now all gone. They disappeared in a single wagon track back to the east. How could things change so quickly?

He scanned the field and could see how well his crops were doing. Everything that once had the beautiful colors of each passing season now had only the shades of black and gray. The trees had been removed for the planting of the wheat in anticipation of a much larger crop—a crop that would have supported Jed and Rose. That had been their plan.

Jed envisioned a garden off to the west of the house. They had talked about what they would grow. She wanted a lot of flowers—roses, marigolds, dahlias, and daisies. He had even dug the well close to where the garden would be so that Rose would not have to carry the water so far.

Jed's eyes focused to the south of the house and there stood the clothesline. He had placed it close to the lean-to so that it would be handy for the washing. He imagined her frilly things blowing on the lines in the breeze. And on these prairies there were a lot of breezes. Sometimes the wind blew strong, blowing anything not hammered down to a new location on the farm.

His mind was full of Rose. Perhaps, he should take off after her and start up a new life out east. Should he go out and bring the family back? He had none of those answers, although his heart was ready to take him wherever she was. Reality slowly brought Jed back and he knew that he needed to stay here just as much as Rose needed to be where she was. If only they had been married before her family had left. Then, together, they could have made plans regarding Wilhelm. That would have been his job as the head of the family. Rose would have listened to him. But, until they were married, that was Rose's mother's decision. He didn't like that but he had to respect her choice.

Then, taking longer than necessary, Jed finished his chores and walked in the twilight to the house. Each step seemed to cry out her name. Everything that he saw, even as the dark was creeping over the farm, reminded him of Rose.

He stood on the porch and felt a wave of lonesomeness and total despair wash over his body. The beautiful auburn beauty, with whom he wanted to share love with, laughs with, and his life with, were gone. He would miss her smile and her laughter.

He walked into the dark front room and pulled out a chair. For the first time that day he allowed himself the luxury of letting his body give up to his emotions. He covered up his face with his big, calloused hands and for the first time since he was a boy, he wept.

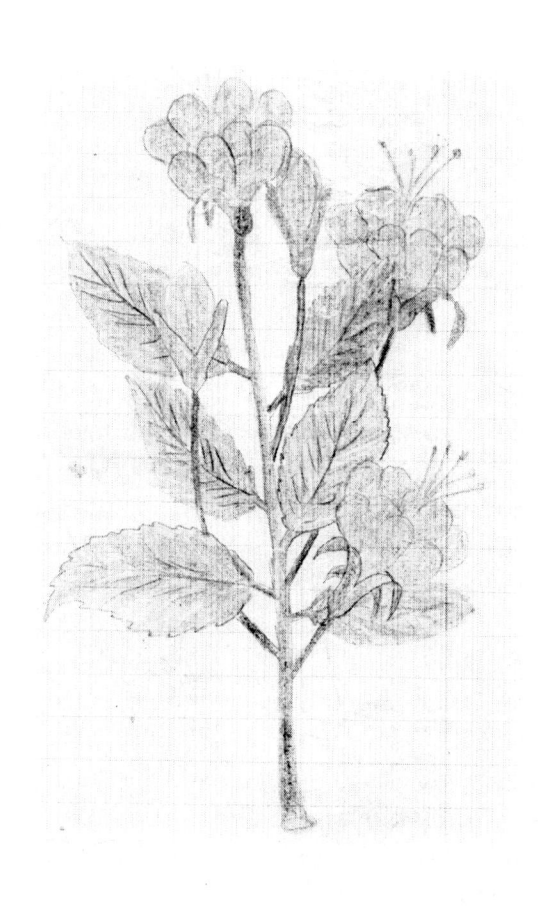

Chapter 8

Many, many times Jed packed up his horse ready to ride to the east to find Rose. But, each time he also unpacked and put his meager supplies away that he had prepared to take with him on his journey. They were laid aside, along with the thoughts of joining her. What would happen to his homestead? It would be too much for his father to care for, and Jake was still too young to watch things. There was always something to do on the farm. No, it was his responsibility alone to maintain his life here. Out east seemed like a long ways, and two hundred miles on horseback would be nearly impossible, especially if he wanted to bring back Rose and her family.

Days turned into months, which, in turn, became a year. Each morning was a struggle for Jed as he woke up to another empty day. He was a successful young farmer but he missed Rose so much that he quit going over to his family's home for Sunday dinner. He no longer went to church or any school functions. He couldn't stand to see the pity on the people's faces. All the eligible women stayed away from him because

Lancaster's Rose

his face was like a storm cloud. Not one of them thought they could equal Rose in his eyes. None of them wanted to be a second love to the man they married.

After a time, Benjamin went to see his son. Oh, he had been there many times, but he waited until he thought he could reason with Jed to talk about Rose.

"Jed, you are going to have to get on with your life. You are working yourself to death on this farm, and for what?"

"I'm hoping that she'll be back."

"As difficult as this might be, you need to find someone with whom to share your life. Rose would not have wanted you to stop living."

"I am living. Each day I wake up I think this is the day she might come back."

"Jed, be realistic. If she were able to come back she would have told you by now."

Jed shrugged.

She had to endure circumstances that most people don't have to deal with. She has huge responsibilities by having to take care of her mother and Hope. She has lost her father and is probably living with relatives, or has a job supporting her mother, Hope, and herself."

"But I could have helped her! Why didn't she let me?"

"You have to face that. She made a choice that she felt was good for her family and you need to respect her for that. You can't spend your life moping about and living from day to day."

Jed knew that he hadn't been the most pleasant person to be around. As much as he did not want to hear what his father said, he knew deep down that he had to make a change in his life. But, how does one forget about a love that penetrated so deep he felt as if he couldn't breathe?

He looked at his father and said, "But how do I do that? None of the girls around here hold a candle to Rose."

"Jed, at this point I think you're right. No young woman around here would equal Rose."

"She was going to be my partner in life. I love her more than I can ever think of loving anyone else. It wouldn't be fair to any woman that I may meet."

"You might be surprised."

"I will always think of Rose and wish I were with her instead."

Benjamin patted his son on the back. "Maybe Rose has a reason for not contacting you."

"She loved being out on the farm."

"Maybe she got back to the city and found a reason to stay there."

"I can't believe that she likes it there. Is she happy among all of that? Why does she stay?"

"Jed, there are some questions that have no answers and there are questions that have answers that we don't like. Perhaps she has found a way to take care of Hope and their mother."

Jed had never thought that Rose might marry someone else. Sure, people married for necessity. Often marriages were arranged. He didn't know if couples would be happy, but maybe they had learned to love one another. Could she love again? Would Rose ever be just a mere thought in his mind? Could he find love again?

"Are you suggesting that I marry someone I don't love?"

"No, Jed. Marriages that are not performed in love often make it miserable for everyone involved. But, sometimes, there are interesting ways to meet people. Arranged marriages sometimes work. Have you heard of a mail order bride? They're becoming more popular."

"How do I go about it? I have heard of mail-order brides but that seems pretty chancy."

His father laughed. "Yes, it does. But I have been speaking to your mother and she agrees that it is time for you to do something."

"Great! I suspect a conspiracy."

Ben laughed. "Hear me out, son. Every month the *Pioneer Press* comes in the mail to the store. I'll pick it up and bring it to you."

"You mean I would advertise for a wife?"

"There is a section for such things. You can look over the personal ads that the young women place. If one of them sounds as if she might be right for you, then you correspond."

"I don't like the sound of this."

"Nothing needs to happen right away. After a few months of corresponding, if it sounds as if she might be interesting to meet, she can come out for a visit. Your mother has agreed to have her stay with us at our home."

"How long have you been planning this?"

"Nothing has been planned, Jed. It is only a suggestion. Think about it for a while. That's how I met your mother, you know."

Never in a million years would Jed have guessed that. They always seemed so much in love that he was sure they fell in love in the normal way. Could he find the same kind of love his parents had?

Benjamin smiled at the reaction on Jed's face. "Yes, son, it is possible. Your mother stepped off of the stage and I was smitten forever."

"I often wondered why she was out here alone."

"It seemed as if I was living and loving a dream. Each day I wake up and look at your mother and watch her sleep. My heart is so full of love that I can't imagine what my life would have been without her."

"Ok, so it worked for you."

"We didn't always have it so easy with trying to break the sod and make a living."

"Did she help you right from the start?"

"From day one, Jed. She pitched everything from hay to manure the first week after we got married."

Jed chuckled. "I can see her doing that."

Lancaster's Rose

"Then you children started to show up and more responsibilities were added to our load. She has had to work hard. We both have had to. But, for us, the marriage did work. And I think that it might work for you."

"It seems risky. What if she gets out here and I don't like her or she's not pretty?"

"At least give it a shot and see what happens. It is not something that you need to commit to right now. I am just saying that many of the east's young ladies might like to be a part of a growing world. You would be a great catch."

Jed smiled in spite of himself. What would he have to lose? He needed to spend some time thinking about this.

And think about it he did. His mind ran the full circle of deciding to go ahead with the process and then totally, in the next moment, become frustrated with the idea. Often finding himself by the stream, Jed drew strength from his memories of his and Rose's times there together. In his mind he would cry out to her, and he had eventually given up on hearing from her again. He still missed her and was sure that he would never forget her. But, his father was right. He had to get on with his life.

By the time Jed had made up his mind another five months had passed. A newspaper was a coveted item and the Fallmans were unsure of who finally ended up with it. So Jed began a waiting game.

He began to take notice of his claim again. As he looked around he saw that he had let things slide a bit. He had lacked the motivation that Rose had given him. He could see how much she had encouraged him to make changes here and there in preparation of their life together.

With these thoughts constantly on his mind, Jed had set about with a new vision and a hope that he would meet someone like Rose. He added a lean-to on the south end of the stable for the buggy and he kept it shiny and smooth looking. He had driven it only once behind the horses and that was to bring it home from town. It would stay in the shed for a long time.

Jed started to go back to his parents' home for Sunday dinners. He missed his mother's cooking and the time that he used to spend with his family. Eventually, he joined them in the family pew. That brought back many memories of what should have happened about a year ago.

The town of Lancaster had changed since Rose left. Doc Mailer had died and a new younger doctor with a wandering eye came to join the small, thriving town. He married Rose's best friend from school and they were soon to have their first baby.

There was a small newspaper office that opened. Even though it was mostly gossip, it was well received by both men and women of the town. The printer's wife had an ear for the untruth, and often her column was the talk in the whispered groups in the church and not so whispered talk in the saloons. Many times a fight broke out because of what

Lancaster's Rose

was said in regards to someone's wife. But at least it provided an interesting twist to the life of Lancaster.

People were always coming and going and the town continued to blossom as gossip of the railroad coming through excited the townspeople. Shopkeepers talked of expanding their stores with visions of a broader spectrum of goods they would be able to sell. The church was full each Sunday, even though Parson Jones was still around. He felt that his calling to the area was as strong as it had ever been. The only one who agreed with his life's calling was his poor mother.

Yes, Jed thought, Lancaster had changed, and, in a way, so had he. As a result of loving Rose, he realized how wonderful love could be. As Jed continued to ponder his father's suggestion, he went through the full gamut of possibilities. What if Rose came back after he was married? What if he did find someone he wanted to spend the rest of his life with? What if he didn't like any of them? Would he settle down with one of them just to have a wife and family?

As promised, Benjamin brought Jed a copy of the *Pioneer Press*. Jed took it to the stream so he could sit by himself and read the ads. Some of the ads were interesting. One wanted to come west and travel to Oregon to begin a new life there. No, that wasn't for Jed. He wanted to stay near Lancaster.

The next one wanted to bring her sister. The young bachelor could meet them both and choose one for his wife and the other sister would live with them. Not for Jed.

Yet, another wanted five hundred dollars for her aging parents and in return would come out and marry any young man who would pay her the money. *Hmm, not likely*, thought Jed. *I'd probably never see my money or the girl.*

Then, in the bottom right-hand corner of the page, the ads took an interesting twist. Any eligible man could write a request for a wife. He could include any traits about himself he wished for a young woman to know. *Well, that certainly sounded interesting*, mused Jed. What does one say when advertising for a wife? He would have to think about that for a while.

And think he did. He sat up far into the nights to ponder what characteristics he wanted to share about himself. He made lists about what he wanted in a wife. Each time he came up with a list he knew he was describing Rose. Was this going to be fair to whichever girl answered his AD?

After much thought and many tossed aside crumples of paper, Jed finally came up with a suitable AD.

> Wanted: for the possibility of marriage, a young woman between the ages of eighteen and twenty-two for a life with a farmer from Lancaster, Iowa. She needs to be a willing partner in the trials of farm life. She must be pretty with auburn hair. A beautiful smile and a sense of humor is a must. Respond to J. Carlson—Lancaster, Iowa.

Lancaster's Rose

Jed reread it and was very pleased. Not too demanding, but it still had some of the necessary requirements that were needed in order to fulfill his expectations. He shared it with his mother, who, with a critical eye, said, "Jed, it sounds as if you are advertising for Rose."

"I can't help it. I know you are right, but this is what I want for a wife."

"Jed, you are setting yourself up for a big disappointment. Do you need more time in order for the hurt of Rose to go away?"

"No, it is better this way. I need to get on with it."

She looked at him and smiled. "You might be surprised when you receive some replies."

"Replies? Do you think I will get more than one?"

That thought had never occurred to him. He didn't like the prospect of a barrage of women writing him. Would he have to write them all back? He had labored so over this letter. What would the people of the town think? They would all know what he was up to. This was getting to be more complicated than he thought. How in the world was he ever going to live down the people's reactions and comments to what he was about to do? If Mrs. Wenter, the town gossip, ever found out, this whole thing would be blown out of proportion.

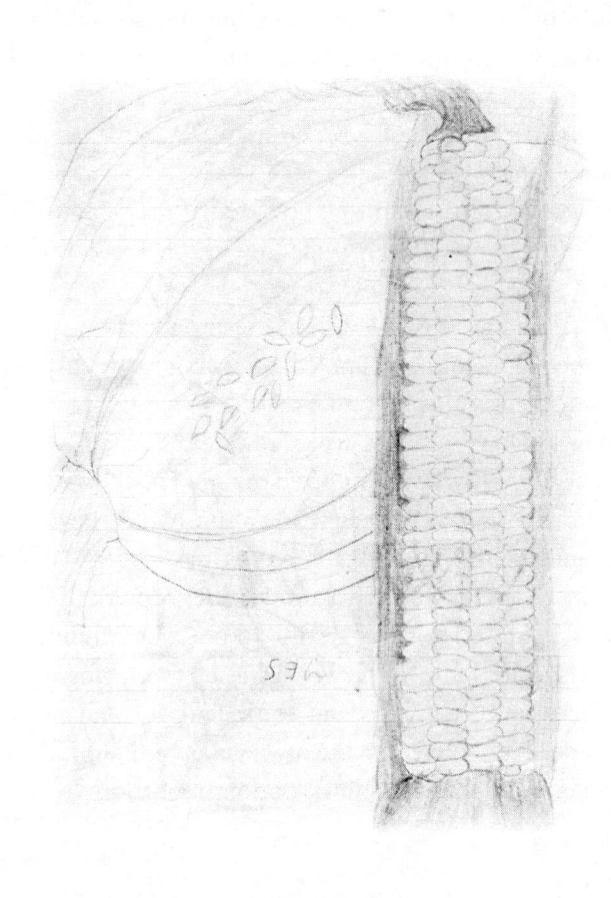

Chapter 9

As busy as Jed managed to keep himself, he was anxious to hear something—anything—as a result of his attempt to get a mail order bride. He feared going into town each week on his pilgrimage to the General Store for the mail. Even though he hadn't told anyone, other than his family, about his plans, he felt as if the entire town were watching him. He couldn't help but wonder what type of woman would answer his AD. Each week he hoped there would be a response from an interested young lady, but he was still fearful that someone would actually answer it.

After nearly two months, a letter arrived on the mail stage. It was from a woman whose husband had died. She had four little boys whom, she said, were so quiet that you could hardly tell that they were around. She was twenty-four and was willing to try a life in the west where she would be able to get away from the city.

He shared this response with his mother.

"I think that she sounds very pleasant. I'd get grandkids right away."

He was surprised that she thought it sounded as if the young lady was a hard-working woman. "Mother, this is about me not you. I don't want a ready-made family."

"Don't be afraid to meet one or two of them."

The second letter came after another month. This one was already married and she was trying to flee her husband who was an abusive sort, only when he drank, which was most of the time. No one needed to know that she was already married. Jed thought at least she was honest, but she hadn't met the likes of Mrs. Wenter.

Jed didn't bother to correspond. He couldn't imagine trying to foster any type of relationship with either woman. This was more difficult than he thought. Why are women such as Rose so difficult to find? He was aware that it might take a while, but he was hoping that he would be lucky.

Several more inquiries came, including the one from the woman who had advertised previously. She and her sister were still willing to travel to Jed and give him a chance to choose one of them and have the other sister live with them. Jed just shook his head and threw the letters into the flames of the fire where the rest of them had gone. He decided this wasn't for him and that was that. No more would he advertise. If he didn't fall in love naturally then he would spend the rest of his life by himself. Bachelorhood couldn't be all that bad. After all, Edward and William, brothers who had always lived together, shared the same house on a neighboring claim for more than forty years. They were together so much that

Lancaster's Rose

Edward could start a sentence and William could finish it for him.

So, when the crops were once again gathered and the little house was tightened down for the winter, Jed began the long evenings at home. Firewood was stacked, apples were tucked away, and vegetables and preserves from his mother's gardens were stocked in the underground root cellar. Jed felt that the only thing missing was Rose. He still thought of her often. Now, when the hands were idle, the brain was very busy. And busy it was. He constantly questioned himself, whether he should have gone after Rose. Was she happy where she was? It had been over a year and a half since she had left. He wondered if she still thought of him.

December was such a cold and dreary month that Jed went nowhere. He had fastened a rope to his house that led to the horse shed just in case a blizzard came up while he was with the animals. Snowstorms came with such a vengeance that, even though Jed had never been afraid, he was glad when they were over. He often came in with snow that had driven into the creases of his outer clothing. Carefully, he would take off the overalls and shake them in the lean-to. He would hang them on a rack close to the stove. He would stomp as much snow off of his boots as possible. Then, he would wonder why he did. He had only been careful because of what Rose would say if he tracked snow into their house with his clunky boots. Now it didn't matter. He tried to feed his horses around noon so that he would only have to feed and water them once daily, especially during the blizzards. But he began to question why he did that. Time passed more quickly if he did chores more than once a day. Sometimes it took over two hours to get what few chores he needed to do done.

Christmas came with no ceremony. The weather was so bad that Jed did not dare venture the three miles to town for Christmas Eve services or to his parents on Christmas Day. He had gotten to see Sophie's amazement the previous year at the tree that was put up in the church. Hanging from the bare branches were treats for everyone. Popcorn balls that were made by the Ladies' Society were wrapped in a mosquito type of netting. There were sacks of apples from Edward and William's apple orchard. Kids and adults of all ages were all aglow with good thoughts and a sense of richness as they divided up the goodies surrounding the tree.

Even though Jed had been there last year, he felt no loss at having to miss this year's service. He sat by the fireplace he had built for Rose and stared into its flames for a long time. Finally, he got up and went to look at the bedroom he and Rose would have shared. He had done this nightly since Rose left. He was not sure of why he did this, but perhaps, in the back of his mind, he hoped that she would be lying there, gently breathing as she slumbered. Lingering only a moment, he backed out of the room and shut the door softly behind him. He, once again, went to lie down on the small bed in front of the stove and slowly his eyes grew heavy, his mind grew weary, and he fell asleep.

So, without realizing it, spring was here and it was time to prepare his farm for the rush of getting the crops into the field. The seed oats were stacked neatly in a corner of his house. He had wanted to keep a watchful eye on it so the small rodents wouldn't carry it away during the winter. The seeds for the corn were stored in one corner of the horse shed, carefully guarded by Molly, the mother cat, and her now five big kittens. They were all sleek and fat from the mice and the rats that they caught over the winter. At least they were self-sufficient and no money went for their upkeep. They protected the seed as well.

The horses had weathered well also. They were ready to hit the pasture and frolic about, munching green grass and wild clover. Jed had known that the mare would foal soon so he was glad when the first signs of spring showed up early.

As he surveyed the walls of the shed, he thought that perhaps he could add some nesting areas for more chickens that he wanted to raise. The coop wasn't big enough. This would be a good year to do just that. More fresh eggs would be mightily welcomed after a hard winter of living on pancakes. He would still have to rely on his mother's fresh produce for next year. Happy with those thoughts, he went about mending the broken down rails of the pasture that had been damaged from the winter's storms.

He was approaching mid-day when he decided that he would ride over to the family farm and get a good home-cooked meal after a lean winter. He had noticed his work trousers fitting a bit loosely. Jenny would see how much thinner he was and would question him on how well he had cooked over the winter. Knowing that a reprimand was coming, he headed to the folks' homestead, anticipating a meal of beef or chicken. It didn't matter. Whatever it was, he would eat it with a great deal of enthusiasm. He could almost taste the juices of the meat rolling over and over his tongue, along with some fresh asparagus, which was always an early spring arrival in April.

So off he went with Prince at a happy trot. Even the horse was ready to exercise his long legs after being cramped up in the horse shed. Right away he headed for the creek for a fresh drink of water. Jed let him take the lead. The day was balmy and bright. It made him feel as if he could never be cross again. The birds were all busy with their nest making and the squirrels were scolding them when the nests were built too close to their liking. Apple buds sent forth their aromatic smells as they flowered with all their might. Green grass grew off the worn path that Jed and his horses had made throughout the last few years.

Almost before he knew it, he was at the homestead. Sophie saw him coming and she screamed with delight, drawing the rest of the family to the door.

"Mama, Jed's home!"

As Sophie leaped into his arms, he saw how much she had grown over the winter. Just as he had anticipated, Jenny scolded her son over how thin he had become.

Lancaster's Rose

"Jed! Have you been eating well? You've had plenty of food down the cellar in the fall to feed you well."

Benjamin happily clasped Jed's outstretched hand and slapped him on the back.

"Good to see you again, Jed. I've been meaning to ride over to your place to see if you were still kicking. Come on in and let's put some meat back on your bones."

Mary yelled through the open window. "Jed, it's about time you came for a visit!"

"Jed, I'm not going back to school when I turn fourteen. I'll be working on the farm and too busy to go to school." Even Jake had grown. His voice was a higher pitch but everything must take its place in due season.

At that last remark Jenny looked at Ben. "Did you tell him he could do that?"

"Not in so many words. I told him if he could read well and cipher sums then we'd talk about it."

"Jed, Mary has a beau."

"Freddy, you have no right to say that. He's not my beau. We've only gone walking a couple of times."

"Yeah, but you look in the mirror a whole lot."

With everyone trying to talk, Jed had trouble keeping up with all of the conversations.

He found that life had continued on for the Carlson family and he had missed them a great deal over the cold, winter months. He lingered at the farm for a while after enjoying his mother's fried chicken and dumplings. Oh, had he ever missed this!

"Did the mare foal yet, Jed? The baby that my horse Lady had, was born two days ago. Father says I may have it to raise and train if I take care of it." Jake was excited over that prospect.

"I was your age, Jake, when I raised my first foal. It was a lot of work but it was worth it."

"What happened to the horse, Jed?"

"I still have it. It's Prince."

The men stepped outside to look over the crops starting to make a stand in the field.

"It looks as if the wheat will do well this year, Jed. In the twenty some years that your mother and I have been on this farm, we've only had one crop failure."

"I don't remember that."

"No, you wouldn't," replied his father. "It was our second year out here and it was almost our last. Grasshoppers came from nowhere and nearly every farmer was wiped out. A lot of homesteaders couldn't make it until spring so they went back east where the jobs were. Lancaster almost died before it started."

"What did you do?"

"Everything and anything I could. We were just in the second year of homesteading and we felt as if we needed to try it one more year and then make up our mind about going back east."

Lancaster's Rose

"Well, then it looks as if the next year was a better one 'cause you're still here."

"Fortunately, it was because we've been here since."

Jake showed the baby horse to Jed and proudly stroked the young animal.

"She's going to be a beautiful horse, and I'll bet a fast one too."

Jed laughed. "What makes you say that?"

"Just look at Lady. She is a great horse. The foal might even be a racehorse."

So, leaving Jake to dream his dreams, Jed and his father walked back to the house where Jed said his goodbyes to his family.

His mother waved and said, "Don't stay away so long next time, Jed."

He nodded his head in acknowledgment and mounted his horse. Turning toward the lane he galloped away.

He decided to make a trip into Lancaster as long as he was this far. There were a few things that he needed to pick up. Some salt pork would taste good and he was nearly out of coffee. While he was at it, he got sugar, flour, soda, and a sack of beans. He figured that boiling some beans should not be that big of a chore. He wasn't sure when to put in the soda, but he thought he saw his mother add it right before the beans started to boil over.

On the way home he stopped by the creek and tied Prince to some willow branches. He sat on one of the bigger boulders and skipped a few pebbles into the stream. He had taught Rose how to do that and he smiled at the recollection of it. He had been daydreaming for quite awhile when his horse's whinny brought him back to reality. The sun was low in the sky and he jumped up and mounted the horse, anxious to get home and do the chores.

Nearly a week later when he was working on repairing a fence, he noticed a rider coming up along the edge of his property. He stood up to get a better view and soon saw that it was Jake.

"What's up, Jake? What are you doing out here in the middle of the day?"

"Mama wanted me to tell you that the stage is coming in this afternoon. There is someone coming to see you on the stage."

"What do you mean?" asked Jed.

"I think that someone answered your letter in the *Pioneer Press*."

Jed had not thought about that for so long that he panicked. "But I am not interested in that anymore. I haven't corresponded for a long time. Why didn't she tell me herself when I was there last week?"

"Well, the letter came in over the winter. Mr. Fallman, at the General Store, gave it to Mama. She has had the letter since December. It said that whoever wrote the letter would be here on the stage in April, besides, the letter was addressed to Mama. The lady had sworn Mama to secrecy."

Lancaster's Rose

"Do you know who the letter was from? "

"No, she only showed it to father and he wouldn't tell either. It's a lot of fuss over a girl if you ask me."

That sounded really strange to Jed. But his mother did know that he would have worried and stewed about it all winter. Why would anyone send a response to his mother? The whole thing didn't sound right.

"What time does the stage come in?" Jed asked.

"It'll be here about three o'clock," Jake answered.

Looking at his timepiece, Jed, clearly bothered by the turn of events, replied, "I don't have time to make myself decent."

"That's another thing Mama said. You are to put on your good clothes. You need to make a good impression."

So Jed, in a much-irritated manner, stomped up to the house and washed up. He put on his Sunday best and slicked down his hair. Feeling grumpy that he had this predicament placed before him, he didn't wait for Jake to mount his own horse before taking off. He thought of how he would let her down gently and send her back on the same stage as she came in on. What nerve she had to write his mother! He wondered if she would be disappointed or cry. He hated it when women cried.

After Jake caught up with Jed, they rode side by side for about half of the way. Then he sent Jake ahead of him. He wanted to stop at the stream. He carefully sat down as to not get mud on himself. This whole mail order bride thing was a mess from the start. To think that his parents encouraged it made it seem even worse. Based on his experience Jed thought that his parents were just plain lucky when they met twenty-two years ago.

He thought of heading back to the farm and forgetting the whole thing. It would serve all of them right. But he thought again of his mother and how disappointed she would be if he didn't at least show up. *Oh, bother!* Already his life was complicated with just the presence of a woman. Hopping back on the saddle, he aimed the horse toward town and let his horse lead the pace.

Unfortunately, when one wants the time to hurry it refuses to and when one wants time to slow down, it hurries. He was soon at the hitching post of the General Store.

"Oh, Jed!"

He turned his head toward the voice and tried not to visibly grimace, but he was unable to help it. It was Mrs. Wenter.

"Good afternoon, Jed. It is such a beautiful day. Are you excited for the stage to get here?"

Oh great, he thought. *She must know, but how?*

"I'll bet you're wondering," she continued in a high-pitched voice, "just how I know about the stage coming in with a special package for you. I have a nose for news so I find out these things."

Jed's ears reddened at the thought of Mrs. Wenter knowing his business. "And just how did you find out?" Jed said with a noticeable edge to his usually calm voice.

Lancaster's Rose

"Oh, I just happened to be in the General Store when the letter came for your mother," she purred. "She dropped it and I scooped it up and read it before she could get it back from me. I didn't get to see who it was from, however. There are tricks to all the trades and my trick is being in the right place at the right time. But, whoever is coming on the stage is mighty glad to see you."

"Mrs. Wenter, do you think that you could just let me deal with this business of the stage and keep your nose out of it?"

She just smiled and said, "We newspaper people have tough skins so you can't hurt my feelings. I'll just be at the newspaper office looking from the window. Have a good day, dear."

Clearly disgusted, Jed turned on his boot heel and looked toward the street.

He noticed that a crowd had been gathering around the blacksmith's shop. They were looking at him and many smiled broadly. He hated to be the center of anyone's attention. On the corner of the General Store's porch he saw his mother waving a hand at him. In a way, he was upset with her. At this point, however, his rage was aimed at Mrs. Wenter. He stomped up the steps and allowed Jenny to pull him into the empty store.

"Jed, I am so sorry. Mrs. Wenter has blown this all out of proportion. It was my fault that she saw the letter. I hated to keep it from you all of this time, but I promised that I wouldn't tell you."

"Mother! Why didn't you tell me?"

"Oh Jed, I wanted too! It was the hardest five months of my life. It was a good thing the weather was bad. At least I didn't have to keep the truth from you every time I saw you."

"How am I going to handle this? Look at all of the people out there! Don't they have anything better to do than pry into my business? And what about the poor girl who is going to get sent right back on the very stage and on the very same afternoon she arrives?"

"Oh Jed, you can't think about that right now. The stage will be here in fifteen minutes. The girl will probably die of embarrassment if you did that."

"Mother, what about me and how I feel? I'm going to be on the front page of Lancaster's gossip column. No self-respecting girl will look at me again. The men and the women will all snicker behind my back. I'll have to go to the farm and never come back to town again!"

"Jed, I know that it looks ridiculous now, but it will blow over soon. See, the people are milling around the town. This will soon be forgotten. You'll have to trust me, son."

Jed's heart sank. What if this woman had no other place to go? He glanced at his mother out of the corner of his eye. She seemed to be enjoying this. Another quick glance and he saw his father trying to fit in with the crowd at the blacksmith's. Was he in on this, too?

Just when he thought it couldn't get any worse, Parson Jones strolled into the store and said, "I hear there's going to be a wedding."

Lancaster's Rose

Jenny hurried Jed outside.

Fifteen minutes had passed in a hurry. Mrs. Wenter was now standing outside the newspaper office. She peered into the distance with her eagle eyes and shouted, "There it is! The stage will be here in just a moment."

Jed looked off in the direction of the stage and saw a cloud of dust following the wooden wheels. More people kept looking out through the store windows. Everywhere he looked there were people peeking out of the windows of the stores. Even the saloon had faces pressed to the window glass. He saw the parson walking up to the church.

What are they doing? mused Jed. *They are taking an awful lot for granted. People are just plain snoopy. It will be worth it to see the looks in their eyes when she gets back on the stage.* He was beginning to feel comfortable with that thought.

The stage stopped in a hurry. Before Jed could open the door of the stage, the driver hopped down and said to Jed. "This is my job, sonny. You can escort her from here. But until they are out of my stage, they are my responsibility."

"They?" asked Jed.

"Yep, she's a downright pretty lady with a young one on her lap."

Okay, thought Jed. *This is how it could be worse, a baby to boot. No one would blame me now if I sent her packing on the next stage.*

The coachman reached up into the luggage compartment high above the stage and tossed down a couple of cases to Jed,

115

nearly knocking him over. He sat them close to the porch of the store. Then, the driver reached up into the passenger compartment and took down a little girl who wasn't a baby but a toddler about two years old, with the most beautiful hair and brown eyes. Jed's heart skipped a beat as he could remember the only other girl he had ever seen with those features.

The driver handed the little girl to Jenny. He turned around again to the stage to help the young woman down. She stepped carefully backward down the steps. She turned around with her big bonnet that had fallen over her face. As the bonnet slid up so did her smile. Jed's face broke into a grin that no one had seen for quite sometime.

"Rose! You're here! How—what happened?" But before he let her answer, he swept her off of her feet and swung her around. When he finally let go she was breathless.

"Oh, Jed, I am really sorry that this had to be such a secret."

"Why didn't you tell me you were coming? I could have helped you somehow."

"At first, I was afraid to write. What would I have done if you had found someone else already? I swore your mother to secrecy."

"Well," said Jed, "you sure picked a good person to trust your secret to. I didn't have a clue about it all before two hours ago."

"I was hoping that would be the case."

He looked into the stage. "Where is your mother?"

Lancaster's Rose

At this Rose turned sober. "You know that Papa died soon after we arrived in Chicago."

"Rose, I'm so sorry. That must have been so difficult for the three of you."

"Yes, Mama tried but after her stroke she gave up and she died about nine months ago."

"Rose, I wish you had let me know."

By the time I got everything sorted out and got Mama's bills paid, I had no money left to come back here on. So I wrote Jenny and asked for her help."

Hmm, thought Jed, *mother had a lot of secrets about this whole thing.*

"She wired me the money. Since Hope is so little she sat on my lap the entire trip. She didn't need a ticket."

Jed continued to look at Rose. He hoped that this wasn't a dream.

"So, here we are. Hope and I. We are a packaged deal. Is it okay for us to still have that home together as we had planned, the three of us?"

If Jed could have jumped over the store he would have. Jed answered her by throwing his hat into the air and pulled Rose to him as if to never let her go.

Suddenly, all the anger for Mrs. Wenter had dissipated. That snoopy old broad had kept the secret only from him! The rest of the town knew. As he glanced around he saw people coming out of every building in town. They were applauding Jed and Rose. Then he remembered Parson Jones's statement about a wedding. He noticed the people heading up to the church. Many of the women carried flowers.

Jed looked at his mother, who said, "Am I forgiven for my part in this?"

Jed hugged his mother in reply.

Benjamin grinned from ear to ear.

"So, you knew the whole time too?"

His reply was only a broader smile.

Turning to Rose, Jed offered his arm, looked at the beautiful woman next to him, and said, "I believe there is going to be a wedding. Shall we?"

"We shall."

And with the rest of the townspeople either already in the church or following the young couple, a wedding with many witnesses and two young people very much in love were married before a man with dry-as-dust sermons.

A cheer went up after the pronouncement of the husband and wife. Mrs. Wenter blew her nose loudly. Jed carried his bride down the steps into his father's waiting carriage. As someone started to hand up Hope to Rose, Jenny stepped forward and said, "Not for a couple of days. She needs to spend some time getting to know her grandma and grandpa."